Suddenly, I felt something moving up my left leg. It advanced gently forward over my chest, stopping just before my chin.

Bending my eyes down as much as I could, I saw a human creature not six inches high with a bow and arrow in his hands and a quiver on his back. In the meantime, what felt like at least forty more of the same creatures followed the first. Completely astonished, I roared so loudly they all ran back in fright . . .

A Background Note about *Gulliver's Travels*

In 1726, when *Gulliver's Travels* was published, explorers were still sailing the seven seas, making discoveries, and capturing the world's imagination with their published accounts. Such tales of great ocean voyages served as models for Swift's completely fictional book. His story is packed with adventure, authentic-sounding details, and convincing observations of faraway lands and people. To the author's delight, some readers actually believed Gulliver's fantastic stories. But Swift's tale was designed to do more than pull the wool over our eyes. In fact, it was intended to help us see more clearly. The author shows the human race at both its best and its worst. He makes us think about our shortcomings while entertaining us with truly extraordinary stories.

JONATHAN SWIFT

GULLIVER'S TRAVELS

Edited, with an Afterword,
by David Kleiner

 THE TOWNSEND LIBRARY

GULLIVER'S TRAVELS

TP THE TOWNSEND LIBRARY

For more titles in the Townsend Library,
visit our website: **www.townsendpress.com**

All new material in this edition is
copyright © 2004 by Townsend Press.
Printed in the United States of America

0 9 8 7 6 5 4 3 2

Townsend Press, Inc.
1038 Industrial Drive
West Berlin, New Jersey 08091

ISBN 1-59194-021-4

Library of Congress Control Number
2003116570

CONTENTS

PART I

A VOYAGE TO LILLIPUT

PART II

A VOYAGE TO BROBDINGNAG

PART III

A VOYAGE TO THE COUNTRY OF THE HOUYHNHNMS

AFTERWORD

GULLIVER'S TRAVELS

PART I

A Voyage to Lilliput

PART I
Chapter 1

My father was not a rich man. He had a small estate in Nottinghamshire. I was the third of five sons. When I was fourteen, I entered Emanuel College in Cambridge. For three years, I applied myself to my studies. But soon, the costs of college grew too great. I left school and became an apprentice to Mr. James Bates, a famous surgeon in London. I stayed with him for four years. At the same time, I was also able to learn navigation and some mathematics. Such knowledge is useful to those who travel. I had always believed that, sometime or another, I would journey about the world.

When I left Mr. Bates, I returned to my father. With his help, and the help of some other relatives, I spent almost three years in Holland continuing my study of medicine. I knew a surgeon's skills are always in demand on long voyages.

Soon after I returned to England, I secured a position as ship's surgeon on the *Swallow*. There I served for three and a half years, voyaging to the Middle East and other places. When I came back, I decided to settle in London. Mr. Bates, my former master, recommended me to several patients. In this way, I was able to start up a private practice. I bought a small house and married Mrs. Mary Burton, second daughter of Mr. Edmund Burton, who made a handsome living selling stockings. He gave us a generous wedding present, a small fortune in cash.

But my good master, James Bates, died two years later. I no longer had someone referring patients to me and my business began to fail. I refused to do as other doctors and take advantage of my clients by overcharging or performing unnecessary surgeries. Instead, I decided to go to sea again. I served as surgeon on two ships and, for six years, made several voyages, including trips to the East and West Indies. I spent my leisure hours reading the best authors, ancient and modern. When ashore, I carefully observed the locals. I studied their culture and language, proving to have a talent for such learning.

Eventually, I grew weary of the sea once more. Intending to stay at home with my wife and family, I moved my business to a port city, expecting to find customers among the sailors. After three years of hoping my business fortunes would improve, I

accepted an offer from Captain William Prichard of the ship *Antelope*, who was making a voyage to the South Seas. We set sail from Bristol, May 4, 1699. Our voyage was—at first—very successful.

Then, misfortune struck. While passing from the South Seas to the East Indies, we were driven by a violent storm to the northwest of Tasmania. Twelve members of our crew had already died from too much work and too little food. The rest were very weak indeed. On the 5th of November, the beginning of summer in those parts, a thick haze obscured the view from the ship. Suddenly, a seaman spied a rock close by, but the wind was so strong that we crashed into it. The boat split apart on impact. Six of the crew—including me—let down a lifeboat and managed, with great difficulty, to get clear of the ship and the rock. We rowed about nine miles. We could row no longer. All we could do next was trust our fate to the mercy of the sea.

In about half an hour, we were overtaken by a sudden storm. The boat capsized. What became of the others in the lifeboat or my companions who were left on the *Antelope*, I do not know. I assume they were all lost. As for me, I swam as well as my limited strength would allow. Just when I was almost completely exhausted, I found I could stand. The storm was nearly over.

I had to walk through the shallows for nearly an hour before I finally reached the shore. I guessed it to be about eight o'clock in the evening. I continued inland for perhaps half a mile, without seeing any sign of houses or inhabitants. Perhaps I was so weak, I simply failed to see them. Needless to say, I was exhausted. That, along with the heat and the half-pint of brandy I drank as I left the ship, put me much in need of sleep. I lay down on my back in the grass, which was very short and soft, and slept more soundly than I had ever done in my life.

I estimate I lay there lifeless for at least nine hours. When I awoke, it was daybreak. I attempted to rise, but was unable to move. I discovered that my arms and legs were solidly fastened to the ground. My hair, which was long and thick, was tied down in the same manner. I likewise felt several slender ropes across my body from my armpits to my thighs. I could only look up. The sun began to grow hot. The light hurt my eyes. I heard a confused noise about me, but could see nothing except the sky.

Suddenly, I felt something moving up my left leg. It advanced gently forward over my chest, stopping just before my chin. Bending my eyes down as much as I could, I saw a human creature not six inches high with a bow and arrow in his hands and a quiver on his back. In the meantime, what felt like at least forty more of the same creatures followed the first. Completely astonished, I roared so loudly that they all ran back in fright. Some of them, I learned later, were hurt leaping to the ground in their panic. However, they soon returned. One brave soul risked approaching close enough to get a full view of my face. His eyes opened wide with awe and he cried out in a shrill but distinct voice, "*Hekinah degul.*" The others repeated the same words several times, but I did not know what they meant. As the reader should appreciate, I was feeling rather uneasy at this point.

Struggling to get loose, I discovered how I was bound. Lifting my arm toward my face, I saw the pegs that had fastened my left arm to the ground. At the same time, with a violent pull (which hurt quite a bit), I loosened the strings that tied my hair down on the left side. I was, at last, able to turn my head, though only about two inches. But the creatures ran off a second time before I could grab one

There was a great shout. A wee voice cried aloud, "*Tolgo phonac.*" In an instant, perhaps a hundred tiny arrows pierced my left hand like so many needles. They followed that volley with another flight of arrows, just as we do with bombs in Europe. I suppose many of them fell on my body, but I did not feel them. I did feel a few on my face, which I immediately covered with my left hand. When this shower of arrows was over, I groaned with grief and pain. When I attempted once again to get loose, they discharged another volley, larger than the first. Some of them attempted to stick spears in my side. Luckily, I was wearing a leather vest, which they could not pierce.

I devised a plan. I would simply lie still until nightfall. With my left arm already loose, I reckoned I could easily free myself. I had every reason to believe, as well, I could defeat an army of these miniature creatures. But fate was against me.

No more arrows flew. But, judging from the noise, many more of the creatures had assembled. About four yards from my right ear, I heard a knocking for more than an hour. Turning my head as best I could, I saw them building something like a stage. It could hold four natives about a foot and a half from the ground. Two or three ladders were placed to allow them to climb onto it. From that stage, one of the creatures, who seemed to be an important person, recited a long speech to me. I didn't understand a syllable.

I should have mentioned that before the oration began, he cried out three times, "*Langro dehul san.*" Immediately, about fifty of the inhabitants cut the strings that fastened the left side of my head. I could now turn and observe the gentleman who was speaking. He appeared to be middle-aged, and taller than any of the other three waiting upon him. The first, whom I estimated to be about as long as my middle finger, was his page. The second and third stood on either side and supported him. As for the speechmaker, he acted very much like orators in our country. Though I could not understand what he said, I could understand what he meant. At times he made threats. At other times he made promises. His gestures expressed pity and kindness.

I answered briefly and meekly in words and gestures. But then, famished with hunger, I let my impatience show a bit. I put my finger to my mouth to indicate that I wanted food. The *hurgo* (for so they call a great lord, as I learned later) understood me very well. Climbing down from the stage, he barked a command. Some ladders were propped against me. No fewer than a hundred citizens climbed up to my mouth. They carried baskets full of meat. The king had ordered that these be provided the moment he learned of my arrival.

There was a variety of meat. I did not recognize the taste of anything. There were shoulders, legs, and loins, shaped like mutton. Each was smaller than a wing of the smallest bird in England. I ate them two or three to a mouthful. I consumed three loaves of bread at a time. Each was the size of a bullet. They supplied me as fast as they could, astonished at my appetite. I then made a sign that I wanted drink. They knew now that a small quantity would not suffice me. These clever folk quickly took one of their largest barrels, rolled it towards my hand, and beat out the top. I downed it in a single gulp. After all, it was less than half a pint and tasted more delicious than Burgundy wine.

They brought me a second barrel, which I drank in the same manner. I made signs for more, but they had none left. When I had performed these wonders, they shouted for joy and danced on my chest, repeating several times as before, "*Hekinah degul.*" They signaled to me to throw down the two hogsheads. They warned the people below to stand out of the way, crying aloud, "*Borach mevolah.*" When they saw the wine casks flying through the air, everyone shouted, "*Hekinah degul.*"

I have a confession. I was tempted, while they were scurrying back and forth across my body, to seize forty or fifty and dash them against the ground. But I remembered the sting of their arrows and wondered if they could do even worse to me. And there was the matter of the promise of honor I made with my previous gestures. Besides, I now considered myself bound by the laws of hospitality. Furthermore, I admired the courage of these pint-sized people. Though one of my hands was free, they ventured out fearlessly onto the body of a giant, before whom they should have trembled.

When they saw that I was no longer demanding food, a person of high rank appeared before me. He climbed up my right leg and proceeded to my face with a dozen followers. He placed his royal credentials close to my eyes. Showing neither fear nor anger, he spoke quite seriously for about ten minutes. He often pointed in the direction—I found out later—of the capital city, about a half-mile away. The Emperor, along with his council, had decided I must be brought there.

I answered briefly but was not understood. I made a gesture with my loose hand (but well above his Excellency's head for fear of hurting him or his attendants) to indicate that I wanted to be freed. It appeared he understood me, for he shook his head in disapproval. Instead, he indicated that I must continue as their prisoner. However, he made other signs to communicate that I would be well fed and gently treated.

I once more thought about breaking the strings that bound me. But the sting of arrows on my face and hands was still fresh in my mind. In fact, some of the arrows were still in my flesh. With the numbers of natives surrounding me increasing, I decided it best to let them do with me as they pleased. As soon as I signaled my submission, a great shout arose, the words "*Peplom selan*" frequently repeated. A large number of wee folk on my left loosened the cords there. Able at last to turn on my side, I immediately proceeded to relieve myself. The people, guessing correctly what I was about to do, parted to avoid the downpour.

Before this, they had daubed my face and both my hands with a pleasant smelling ointment. In a few minutes, it removed all the pain from their arrows. Being relatively comfortable and completely sated with food and drink for the first time in hours, I became drowsy. I slept about eight hours, I was later told. That was not surprising. By order of the Emperor, a sleeping potion had been mixed into my wine.

It seems a special messenger had notified the Emperor the moment I was discovered sleeping on the ground. Everything I've just described had been decided then. I would be tied up in the night while I slept. Plenty of meat and drink would be prepared. A machine was prepared to carry me to the capital city.

To some, this may appear to have been a very bold and dangerous plan. No prince of Europe would have the courage or intelligence to do the same. However, in my opinion, it was both sensible and generous. Suppose these people had tried to kill me with their spears and arrows while I was asleep? I would certainly have awakened with the first arrow. My anger and strength would have enabled me to break the strings with which I was tied. At that point, I would have shown no mercy.

The Emperor had long encouraged his subjects through his support of learning. As a result, his people are excellent mathematicians who can apply their skills. Long before my arrival, they already had constructed several machines—on wheels—for hauling trees and other great weights. The emperor's largest warships—some as long as nine feet—are built in the woods right where the timber grows and then hauled three or four hundred yards to the sea.

Upon my arrival, five hundred carpenters and engineers had immediately set to work building the greatest machine the country had ever known. It was a frame of wood raised three inches from the ground. About seven feet long and four wide, it was set on twenty-two wheels. A shout announced the arrival of this marvel, which had been built in a matter of hours. It was put directly beside me. Everything was now in place for the greatest challenge, lifting me onto the vehicle. Eighty poles, each one-foot high, were erected. Using hooks, workmen fastened heavy-duty cords—similar to the twine we use for packages— to many sturdy cloths. Hundreds of laborers slung these around my neck, hands, trunk, and legs.

Nine hundred of the strongest men were employed to tighten these cords. Each was fastened by pulley to one of the poles. In less than three hours, I was raised onto the vehicle and securely tied. All this I was told later. While the work went on, I had been in a deep sleep, under the influence of the medicines in my liquor.

Fifteen hundred of the emperor's largest horses, each about four inches and a half high, pulled me towards the capital city. As I said, it was a distance of about a half-mile.

About four hours after we began our journey, I awoke due to a ridiculous accident. The vehicle had been stopped for an adjustment of some sort. Two or three of the young natives, curious to see me asleep, climbed up to take a look. They quietly approached my face. One of them, an officer in the guards, put the sharp end of his spear a good way up my left nostril. This tickled my nose like a feather. I sneezed violently. They snuck off before anyone saw them. It was not until three weeks later that I learned what had awakened me so suddenly.

We continued on all day. At night we rested. Five hundred guards stood on each side of me; half held torches. The other half held bows and arrows, ready to shoot me if I should stir. The next morning at sunrise we continued our march and arrived outside the city gates about noon. The emperor and all his court came out to meet us. The assembled ministers would not, however, permit his majesty to risk climbing onto me.

Where we stopped there stood an ancient temple, said to be the largest in the whole kingdom. Ever since someone committed a terrible murder there, it had not been used. The king and his council had declared I would stay in this imposing structure. The great gate on its northern side was about four feet high and almost two feet wide. I could easily creep through it. On each side of the gate was a small window, less than six inches from the ground. There, the king's own blacksmith fastened ninety-one chains, rather like those that hang from a lady's watch in Europe. Using these chains, my left leg was locked with thirty-six padlocks. About twenty feet from this temple, on the other side of the great highway, there was a tower at least five feet high. The emperor climbed it, with many important officers of his court, to look me over. This I was also told later. I could not see them.

More than one hundred thousand inhabitants came out of the town for the same purpose. And, in spite of my guards, I believe no less than ten thousand citizens mounted my body by climbing ladders. But a proclamation was soon issued, forbidding such sightseeing on pain of death.

Convinced it was impossible for me to break loose, the workmen cut all the strings that bound me. I stood up immediately, as downhearted as I had ever been in my life. The chains were about six feet long, allowing me to creep into the temple and lie full length. I discovered I could also walk backwards and forwards in a semicircle. The clamor that arose from the people at seeing me rise and walk is beyond description.

PART I
Chapter 2

When I found myself at last on my feet, I looked all about. I've never seen a lovelier view. The country around me appeared to be one continuous garden. This garden consisted of a series of enclosed fields, each about forty feet square, each like a bed of flowers. Between these fields were scattered forests of about half an acre each. I estimated the tallest trees to be seven feet high. On my left was the town, which looked like the painted scene of a city in a theatre.

For some time, I had been hard-pressed by the necessities of nature. It was no wonder, as it had been almost two days since I had last answered the call. I was under great pressure from my urgency on one side and my shame on the other. Finally, I crept into my house and shut the gate. I went as far as my chains would allow and emptied myself of that uneasy load. I hope the reader will consider my distress and forgive this unclean act. From that day on, as soon as I rose, I performed my business in the open air at the full extent of my chain. Every morning, before company came, two servants (appointed specifically for that purpose) carried off the offensive material in wheelbarrows. Please understand, dear reader, I would have preferred not to include in this account what might seem to some a minor matter. But I felt I had to justify my actions after some critics questioned my cleanliness.

This adventure over, I came back out of my house feeling a need for fresh air. The emperor was riding towards me, unaware of the danger he would face. His stallion, though well trained, was unprepared for the sight of me. I must have appeared like a moving mountain to the animal. He reared up on his hind feet. Fortunately, that prince is an excellent horseman. He was able to stay on the horse until his attendants ran in and grabbed the bridle. Then his majesty dismounted. He examined me with great admiration, carefully keeping himself beyond the length of my chain. He ordered his cooks and butlers to give me food and drink, which they pushed forward in receptacles on wheels. Twenty were filled with meat, ten with liquor. I consumed each container of food in two or three good mouthfuls. I downed the liquor even more quickly.

The empress and royal family, attended by many ladies, sat some distance away. But when the emperor's horse reared, they ran over to him. The emperor is taller than anyone else in the royal court by about the width of my fingernail. When his subjects see him, they immediately marvel at his height. His face is strong and masculine, with thick lips and an arched nose. His complexion is olive, his posture straight, his body muscular yet graceful. By their standards, he was middle-aged, being twenty-eight and three quarters years old. His subjects had always been content and almost always victorious in war during the seven years of his reign.

He stood only three feet away from me. To see him better, I lay on my side. Since then, I have had him in my hand many times. My description of him is, therefore, very accurate. His manner of dress was very plain and simple, with a style somewhere between Asian and European. He wore a light helmet of gold, adorned with jewels and a feather on the top. His sword, almost three inches long, was made of gold inlaid with diamonds. His voice was high-pitched, but clear. I could hear him clearly even when I stood up. His imperial majesty said quite a lot to me, and I answered. However, we could not understand each other. Several of his priests and lawyers (as I guessed from their behavior) approached. His Majesty had commanded them to speak to me. I answered in every language

I knew even a bit of—German, Dutch, Latin, French, Spanish, and Italian. But, alas, we could not make ourselves understood.

After about two hours, everyone left. Only a company of guards remained, probably to keep away the mobs that came to gawk, and even shoot arrows at me, as I sat on the ground by the door of my house. One arrow barely missed my left eye. The colonel of the guard ordered six of the ringleaders seized. Their punishment? Soldiers tied them up and then pushed them close enough for me to grab. I dropped five into my coat-pocket. I made a show of getting ready to eat the sixth. The poor man cried terribly. When I took out my penknife, even the colonel and his officers trembled. They were relieved when I cut the strings binding the prisoner. I set him gently on the ground and away he ran. I treated the rest the same way, taking them out of my pocket one by one. Everyone watching was delighted by my show of mercy. My standing with the emperor rose greatly when the story reached the royal court.

At nightfall, I managed to crawl into my house. There I slept directly on the cold floor. I did so for two weeks during which time the emperor gave orders to have a bed made for me. Six hundred of their beds were brought in carriages and carried into my house. A hundred and fifty such beds, sewn together, made up each of four layers of my mattress. Even so, I felt as if I were lying directly on smooth stone. They likewise provided me with sheets and blankets. All in all, the arrangement was sufficient for a man accustomed to hardship.

As the news of my arrival spread through the kingdom, huge crowds of the rich, the out of work, and the curious came to see me. Whole villages were almost emptied. Farming and housekeeping were being neglected. At last his imperial majesty issued several proclamations. He ordered that anyone who had already seen me must return home. No one was allowed within fifty yards of my house without a special license. The fees enriched the royal treasury and the pockets of many government workers.

Meanwhile, the emperor convened councils to debate what should be done with me. A friend later informed me secretly that I posed a thorny problem for the state. They feared I might break loose. They worried that my diet would be very expensive and could even cause a famine. At one point they decided to starve me or at least shoot me in the face and hands with poisoned arrows. However, they realized that the stench of such a large corpse might cause a plague in the city that would probably spread through the whole kingdom. Fortunately, in the middle of these discussions, several army officers testified about my kindhearted treatment of the six criminals. Instead of starving me, an order went out requiring all villages within nine hundred yards of the city to deliver every morning six beef cattle, forty sheep, and other food as well as an enormous quantity of bread, and wine, and liquor. The king paid for everything out of his treasury. In this kingdom, taxes are rarely collected, except during wartime, when all subjects are also required to serve in the army. The king lives on the income from his own lands.

Six hundred servants were hired for me. They were paid a reasonable wage and given tents in which to live. These were placed on either side of my doorway. The king ordered three hundred tailors to make me a suit of clothes in the local style. Six of his majesty's greatest scholars were employed to teach me their language. Lastly, he ordered that all royal and military horses were to be exercised in my vicinity. In this way, they would accustom themselves to me.

All these orders were properly carried out. In about three weeks, I had already made great progress in learning their language. During that time, the emperor frequently honored me with visits. He even assisted my masters in teaching me. We began to communicate. The first words I asked to learn expressed my desire "that his highness would please give me my freedom." This I repeated every day on my knees. His answer, as best I could understand was, "This will take time. It can only be done with the consent of the council. And first you must agree to the terms of a peace treaty with me and my kingdom." He promised I would be fairly treated and advised me to "acquire, by patience and sensitive behavior, a good reputation." He told me, furthermore, not to take it the wrong way if some high-ranking officers were ordered to search me and confiscate my weapons, since these must be quite dangerous if they matched my size.

I humbly answered, "Your majesty will be satisfied. I am ready to strip naked and turn out my pockets for him." This I communicated using words and signs.

He replied, "By the laws of the kingdom, then, two officers will search you." His decision proved his high regard for me. He knew a search could never be done without my consent. He trusted me enough to put two officers of the court into my hands. He further promised that anything they took from me would be returned when I left the country.

I lifted the two officers in my hands, putting them first into my coat-pockets and then into every other pocket about me. I disclosed everything except one secret compartment, which I did not want searched. There I kept some items of importance only to myself. The men who searched made an exact inventory of everything they saw. When they were done, I set them down so they could deliver it to the emperor. I later translated this inventory into English. It is, word for word, as follows:

First of all: After a careful search, we found in the right coat-pocket of the great man-mountain (for so I translate the words *quinbus flestrin*), one enormous piece of cloth, large enough to be a carpet for your majesty's assembly hall. In the left pocket we saw a huge silver chest, with a cover of the same metal, which we, the searchers, were unable to lift. We requested it be opened. One of us stepped in and found himself up to his thighs in some kind of dust. It flew up into our faces causing both of us to sneeze several times. In his right coat-pocket, we found a huge bundle of thin white substances, folded one over another, about the size of three men, tied with a strong cable, and marked with black figures. We believe these to be writing, every letter almost half as large as the palm of our hands. In the left there was a sort of machine, from the back of which were extended twenty long poles. We did not trouble him with questions, because we found it difficult to be understood. In the large pocket, on the right side of his middle cover (so I translate the word *ranfulo*, by which they meant my pants,) we saw a hollow pillar of iron, about the length of a man, fastened to a strong piece of timber larger than the pillar; and upon one side of the pillar were huge pieces of iron sticking out, cut into strange figures, which we did not recognize. In the left pocket, we found another machine of the same kind. In the smaller pocket on the right side were several round flat pieces of white and red metal, of various sizes. Some of the white pieces, which seemed to be silver, were so large and heavy that my comrade and I could hardly lift them. In the left pocket were two black pillars, irregularly shaped. We could not, without difficulty, reach the top of them, as we could only stand at the bottom of his pocket. One of them was covered, and seemed to be a solid piece. At the upper end of the other there appeared a white round substance, about twice the size of our heads. Within each of these was enclosed an immense plate of steel. We ordered him to show them to us, because we thought they might be dangerous engines. He took them out of their cases, and used gestures to show how he used one to shave his beard and the other to cut his meat. There were two pockets we could not enter which he called *fobs*. They were two large slits cut into the top of his middle cover, but squeezed close by the pressure of his belly. Out of the right fob hung a great silver chain, with a wonderful kind of engine at the bottom. We directed him to draw out whatever was at the end of that chain. It appeared to be a globe, half silver and half of some transparent metal. On the transparent side we saw certain strange figures. We thought we could touch them, till we found our fingers stopped by the clear substance. He put this engine to our ears. It made a constant noise, like that of a mill wheel. We conclude it is either some unknown animal or the god that he worships. We are more inclined to believe it is a god, because he told us (if we understood him right, for he expressed himself very imperfectly) that he seldom did any thing without consulting it. He called it his guide and said it pointed out the time for every action in his life. From the left fob, he took out a net almost large enough for a fisherman, but designed to open and shut like a purse. Indeed, that is how he used it. We found inside several substantial pieces of yellow metal, which, if they are real gold, must be quite valuable.

Instructed by your majesty to search everywhere, we noticed a belt around his waist made of the hide of some gigantic animal. From it, hung a sword as long as five men. On the right, we found a pouch divided in two. Each side could hold three of your majesty's subjects. In one compartment were several globes of heavy metal about the size of our heads. Only the strongest man could hope to lift one. The other section contained a heap of black particles. These were quite small. We could hold more than fifty in the palms of our hands.

This is an exact inventory of what we found on the man-mountain. He treated us very politely and showed respect for your majesty's orders. Signed and sealed on the fourth day of the eighty-ninth moon of your majesty's prosperous reign.

CLEFRIN FRELOCK, MARSI FRELOCK

After this inventory was read to the emperor, he directed me, very politely, to give up several items. He called first for my sword. This I took out, scabbard and all. At the same time, three thousand of his best troops surrounded me (at a safe distance) with their bows and arrows ready. I didn't even notice, for my eyes were fixed on his majesty. He asked me to draw my sword. Though it had rusted a bit from salt water, it was still, in some places, quite bright. When I drew it out, the soldiers gave a shout somewhere between terror and surprise. The reflection of the sun dazzled their eyes as I waved the sword back and forth. His majesty, who is a most worthy prince, was less frightened than I expected. He ordered me to place it—in its scabbard—gently on the ground, beyond the end of my chain.

The next thing he demanded was one of the "hollow iron pillars" (pocket pistol). I took it out and, at his request, explained its use. I demonstrated by loading it with powder only. I warned the emperor not to be afraid and then discharged the pistol into the air. The astonishment this time was far greater than at the sight of my sword. Hundreds fell down as if they had been struck dead. Even the emperor, although he stood his ground, did not recover his composure for some time. I delivered up both pistols in the same manner as before and then my pouch of powder and bullets. I begged his majesty to be sure these would be kept away from fire. The smallest spark could set them off and blow his imperial palace into the air.

I also gave up my watch, which the emperor was very curious to see. He commanded two of his tallest guards to bear it on a pole on their shoulders. He was amazed at the steady noise it made and the motion of the minute hand. He asked the opinions of his learned men. Each suggested a different explanation. Each was completely wrong.

I also gave up my silver and copper money, my purse with nine large pieces of gold, my knife and razor, my comb and snuffbox, my handkerchief and my journal-book. My sword, pistols, and pouch were transported in carriages to his majesty's storehouse. Everything else was returned to me.

In one of the pockets that escaped their search, I had my glasses, a pocket telescope, and some other little personal items. I felt these were of no consequence to the emperor and I did not think honor demanded I turn them over. I feared they might be lost or spoiled if I were no longer in possession of them.

PART I
Chapter 3

My gentleness and good behavior had so impressed the emperor and his court that I became convinced my day of liberty was at hand. I did everything I could to curry the favor of the royals. The natives slowly came to fear me less. I would sometimes lie down and let five or six of them dance on my hand. Boys and girls would play hide-and-seek in my hair. I had progressed well toward understanding and speaking the language.

The emperor decided one day to entertain me with several of their shows, which are better than any I have seen in all my travels. I found the rope-dancers the most entertaining of all. They perform on a slender white thread about two feet long and twelve inches from the ground. Only candidates for positions at the royal court take part.

Even commoners and the uneducated practice

this skill from childhood. When an important position becomes vacant, either by death or disgrace (which often happens), five or six candidates entertain the emperor and the court with this dance on a rope. Whoever jumps the highest without falling wins the position. Oftentimes the chief ministers are also commanded to show their skill to convince the emperor they have not lost their talent. Flimnap, the treasurer, is said to leap about on the rope an inch higher than any other lord. I have seen him do several somersaults one after the other on a plate fixed on a rope no thicker than English twine. My friend Reldresal, the emperor's private secretary, is, in my opinion, second best. The rest of the high officers do not compare.

Fatal accidents have been known to happen during the rope dance. A great number are on record. I saw two or three candidates break their legs. The danger is greatest when ministers compete. They try so hard to outdo each other that every one, at one time or another, has fallen. Some have fallen two or three times. I was told that, a year or two before my arrival, Flimnap would have broken his neck if, purely by chance, one of the king's cushions had not broken his fall.

There is another competition held before the emperor, empress, and first minister on special occasions. The emperor places on the table three fine silk threads six inches long. One is blue, one red, and one green. These threads are prizes for those on whom the emperor decides to show favor. The ceremony is performed in his majesty's great assembly hall. The candidates go through a test of dexterity different from anything I have seen anywhere. The emperor holds a stick parallel to the ground. The candidates approach one by one. Sometimes they leap over the stick. Sometimes they creep under it, backward and forward, several times, depending on the position of the stick. The emperor rewards the blue thread to the candidate who proves most agile. The red thread indicates second place, green, third place. The threads are worn wrapped twice around about the middle. Most of the important people at court are decked out with one of these prizes.

The horses of the army, and those of the royal stables, are no longer frightened of me. Indeed, they come up to my feet without shying away. The riders encourage them to leap over my hand, as I hold it on the ground. One of the emperor's huntsmen, on a strong, swift horse, pulled off a remarkable feat. He cleared my foot and shoe in a single bound.

One day, I amused the emperor in an unusual way. I asked that a quantity of sticks two feet high and as thick as an ordinary cane be brought me. My supplies arrived the next morning in six carriages drawn by eight horses each. I took nine sticks and fixed them firmly in the ground in a rectangle two and a half feet square. I took four other sticks and tied them parallel to each other at each corner about two feet from the ground. I fastened my handkerchief to the nine sticks that stood upright. I pulled it all around until it was as tight as the top of a drum. The four parallel sticks, rising about five inches higher than the handkerchief, served as railings on each side.

When I finished, I invited the emperor to let a troop of his best horses exercise on this stage. His majesty approved and I took them up, one by one, mounted and armed, ready to exercise. They divided into two parties and performed simulated battles complete with swords and arrows. The railing kept riders and horses from falling off the stage. The emperor was so delighted that he ordered this entertainment repeated several times. Once, the emperor himself was lifted up to command the training. He even managed to persuade the empress to let me hold her in her chair only two yards from the stage. There, she had the finest seat from which to view the whole performance. Fortunately, no accidents happened until a fiery horse, pawing with his hoof, struck a hole in my handkerchief. His foot slipped, overthrowing rider and horse. I caught them both and, covering the hole with my hand, set the entire troop down. The horse that fell suffered a shoulder strain. The rider was unhurt. I repaired my handkerchief as best I could. However, I could no longer trust its strength for such dangerous activities.

About two or three days before I was set free, a special messenger arrived. He informed his majesty that a great black substance—oddly shaped, as wide as his majesty's bedchamber, and as high in the middle as a man—had been found by some soldiers near where I first appeared. By climbing on each other's shoulders, they had gotten to the top and found it flat and even. Stamping on it, they discovered it was hollow inside. They supposed it might be something belonging to the man-mountain. They proposed to bring it to his majesty with only five horses. I immediately knew what they had found.

Somehow, in the confusion of my coming ashore, I had lost my hat. Fastened by a string to my head, it had stuck with me the whole time I was swimming for dear life. It fell off after I landed. I assumed the hat had been lost at sea. I pleaded with his imperial majesty to order it brought to me as soon as possible. The next day it arrived, though not in good condition. They had bored two holes in the brim and there fastened two hooks. With a long cord, they tied the hooks to a harness. My hat was then dragged along for about half an English mile. Thankfully, because the ground in that country is extremely smooth and level, it received less damage than I expected.

Two days after this adventure, the emperor ordered the divisions of his army guarding the great city to prepare for special maneuvers. He

requested that I stand like a statue with my legs as far apart as I could comfortably manage. He commanded his general (an old experienced leader, and a great supporter of mine) to draw up the troops in close order. He then marched them under me twenty-four abreast. The cavalry rode forward in rows of sixteen with drums beating and colors flying. The entire division consisted of three thousand foot soldiers and a thousand mounted troops.

His majesty gave orders, on pain of death, that every soldier must observe the strictest decency with regard to me. Even a royal order, however, could not prevent some of the younger officers from turning up their eyes as they passed under me. I must confess that my pants were in poor condition at the time. This provided the opportunity for laughter and admiration.

I had sent so many petitions requesting my release that his majesty finally brought the matter up for consideration. First in the cabinet, and then in full council, only Skyresh Bolgolam opposed the petition. He had decided, for some reason, to be my mortal enemy. But the vote carried because everyone else on the board was in favor of the motion. Then, the emperor endorsed their decision. I would have my liberty at last.

Skyresh Bolgolam was chief naval officer of the realm. The emperor trusted him completely. He was knowledgeable, but gloomy. He had no choice but to comply with the decision. He did, however, insist that he should personally prepare the articles spelling out the conditions upon which I would be set free, and to which I must swear. Once they were completed, Skyresh Bolgolam brought the articles to me personally. Two under-secretaries and several important persons came with him. After the conditions were read, I swore to obey them. First I swore in the manner of my own country. Next, I pledged my oath as required by their laws: I held my right foot in my left hand and placed the middle finger of my right hand on the top of my head; at the same time, I placed my thumb on the tip of my right ear.

I know some readers are curious about official Lilliputian documents. Others want to see the articles that restored my liberty. Therefore, I have translated the whole document to the best of my ability. Here, I offer it to the public:

> Golbasto Momarem Evlame Gurdilo Shefin Mully Ully Gue, most mighty Emperor of Lilliput, delight and terror of the universe, whose dominions extend five thousand blustrugs (about twelve miles in all directions) to the extremities of the globe; monarch of all monarchs, taller than the sons of men; whose feet press down to the center of the Earth, and whose head strikes against the sun; at whose nod the princes of the earth shake their knees; his most sublime majesty proposes to the man-mountain, lately arrived at our celestial dominions, the following articles, which, by a solemn oath, he shall be obliged to perform:
>
> 1st, The man-mountain shall not leave our kingdom without official permission.
>
> 2nd, He shall not enter our great city, unless so ordered. At that time, the inhabitants shall be warned, at least two hours in advance, to stay indoors.
>
> 3rd, The man-mountain shall walk only on major roads, and must never walk or lie down in a meadow or field.
>
> 4th, When he walks said roads, he shall take the utmost care not to trample on any of our

subjects, their horses, or carriages. Neither shall he take any of our subjects into his hands without their permission.

5th, If an important message requires speedy delivery, the man-mountain shall be obliged to carry, in his pocket, the messenger and horse a maximum of six days and safely return the said messenger (if so required).

6th, He shall be our ally against our enemies in the island of Blefuscu, and do his utmost to destroy their fleet, which is now preparing to invade us.

7th, The said man-mountain shall, at his times of leisure, help our workmen in the lifting of certain great stones for royal building projects.

8th, The said man-mountain shall, in two moons' time, measure the distance from one end of the kingdom to the other, based on the length of his stride.

Lastly, should he obey all of the above articles, the said man-mountain shall have a daily allowance of meat and drink equal to that which would support 1,724 Lilliputians. He shall also have free access to our royal person, and other signs of our favor. Approved at our palace at Belfaborac, the twelfth day of the ninety-first moon of our reign.

I swore to these articles cheerfully, although some (thanks to Skyresh Bolgolam) were not very honorable. My chains were immediately unlocked, and I was at full liberty. The emperor himself, in person, did me the honor of attending the ceremony. I acknowledged his generosity by bowing at his feet. But he commanded me to rise. After many compliments which modesty forbids me from repeating, he added, "You have already proven to be a valuable servant, and well deserve all the favors conferred upon you, now and in the future."

The reader may have noticed that, in the last article of the recovery of my liberty, the emperor stipulates an allowance for me of meat and drink enough to sustain 1,724 Lilliputians. Later, I asked a friend at court how they calculated that particular number. He told me that his majesty's mathematicians measured the height of my body and found it greater than theirs by a ratio of twelve to one. They then estimated that my body could contain at least 1,724 of theirs. Presumably, I require as much food as is necessary to feed that number of Lilliputians. This gives the reader an idea of the creativity of that people, as well as the careful economic policies of their emperor.

PART I
Chapter 4

The first request I made after I became free was to see Mildendo, the metropolis. The emperor granted my wish after I promised to do no damage to the inhabitants or their houses. A proclamation notified the citizens of my visit.

The wall surrounding Mildendo is two feet and a half high and at least eleven inches wide. It was designed to allow a coach and horses to be driven safely around it. It is flanked with strong towers every ten feet. I stepped over the great western gate and passed very gently through the two main streets. I wore a short coat to prevent damage to houses. Orders were very strict that all people should keep in their houses, at their own peril. Nevertheless, I walked with the utmost care, to avoid treading on any stragglers. Windows and rooftops were crowded with spectators. In all my

travels, I had never seen a more densely populated place. The town is capable of holding five hundred thousand souls.

The emperor's palace is in the center of the city where two great streets meet. A wall of two feet encloses it, twenty feet from any buildings. I had his majesty's permission to step over this wall. The wide space between the wall and the palace enabled me to view it from every side. The outward court is a square of forty feet and includes two other courts. The innermost court holds the royal apartments. These I wanted to see very much but found it extremely difficult. The buildings of the outer court were at least five feet high. As a result, I could not stride over them without doing some damage. But the emperor wanted me to see the magnificence of his palace. Two or three days later, I made it possible.

I cut down some of the largest trees in the royal park. From these trees I made two stools, each about three feet high, and strong enough to bear my weight. The people were warned of my visit a second time. I went again through the city to the palace, this time carrying the two stools. When I came to the outer court, I stood on one stool and held the other. I lifted it over the roof and gently set it down in the space between the first and second court, which was eight feet wide. I then stepped over the building from one stool to the other. I lifted up the first stool after me with a hooked stick. In this way, I got into the innermost court. Lying down on my side, I applied my face to the windows of the middle stories, which had been left open on purpose. There, I saw the most splendid apartments anyone could imagine. I saw the empress and the young princes in their rooms. Her imperial majesty smiled graciously and gave me her hand to kiss.

Someday soon, I plan to write an even longer book that will fully describe Lilliput. I don't want to repeat anything my readers will learn later. So I will end the description of my visit here.

One morning, about two weeks after I was freed, Reldresal, principal secretary for private affairs (as they call him), came to my house. He ordered his coach to wait at a distance and requested an hour of my time. I agreed largely because of the many favors Reldresal had done for me. I offered to lie down so he could conveniently reach my ear. Instead, he chose to let me hold him in my hand. He congratulated me on my newly won freedom. But everything was not well at the royal court. There was a dangerous political party at home, and the risk of invasion by a powerful foreign enemy.

"For about seventy moons," he explained, "there have been two opposing political parties in the empire, the Tramecksan and Slamecksan. The major difference between the two parties is the height of the heels of their shoes. The Tramecksan wear only high heels. The Slamecksan only low heels. Some say that high heels are more in line with our ancient traditions. However, his majesty has decided to make use only of low heels in his government. The hatred between these two parties runs so high that they refuse to eat, drink, or even talk with one another. We believe the Tramecksan party has more members. But we have all of the power.

"Now, in the midst of this internal strife, we

are threatened with an invasion from the island of Blefuscu. Blefuscu is the other great empire of the universe, almost as large and powerful as ours. Our philosophers are in much doubt that there are other kingdoms and states in the world inhabited by human creatures as large as you. They conclude instead that you dropped from the moon or one of the stars. After all, a hundred creatures of your size would, in a short time, destroy all the fruits and cattle in this entire kingdom. Besides, our histories of six thousand moons make no mention of any regions other than the two great empires of Lilliput and Blefuscu. These two mighty powers have been engaged in a war for thirty-six moons.

"It began in this way. Everyone agrees that the ancient way of breaking eggs was on the larger end. His majesty's grandfather, however, while still a boy, was intending to break an egg on the larger end and happened to cut one of his fingers. The emperor, his father, immediately commanded all of his subjects to break the smaller end of their eggs. The people so highly resented this law that six rebellions followed. As a result, one emperor lost his life, another his crown. The monarchs of Blefuscu were happy to support civil unrest in Lilliput. The exiles from uprisings that failed fled for refuge to that empire. Altogether, eleven thousand persons have died rather than submit to breaking their eggs at the smaller end.

"Hundreds of books have been published

about this controversy. In Lilliput, the books of the Big-endians are outlawed. Big-endians are not allowed to hold government positions. The leaders of Blefuscu insist this is a religious question. They cite a passage from our great prophet Lustrog, in the fifty-fourth chapter of the Blundecral (which is their Koran). Lustrog states, 'All true believers break their eggs at the convenient end.' It seems to me, identifying the convenient end is a personal matter, or at the least one to be decided by the emperor. Because of all the Big-endian exiles in the court of the emperor of Blefuscu, a bloody war has been carried on between the two empires for thirty-six moons. We have lost forty great warships and many smaller vessels, as well as thirty thousand of our best soldiers and sailors. The enemy has suffered losses even greater than ours. However, they have now equipped a large fleet and are preparing to attack. His imperial majesty has great confidence in your courage and strength. Therefore, he has commanded me to describe the entire situation to you."

I pledged my services to the emperor and declared, "Though it would be wrong for me, a foreigner, to interfere on my own, I am ready to risk my life to defend his person and state against all invaders."

PART I
Chapter 5

The empire of Blefuscu is an island northeast of Lilliput. A waterway only eight hundred yards wide separates the two. Once I received notice of the intended invasion, I avoided appearing on that side of the coast for fear of being observed by one of the enemy's ships. Blefuscu did not know of my existence. All communication between the two empires was strictly forbidden upon pain of death.

Our spies had assured us the enemy fleet lay anchored at port, ready to sail with the first fair wind. I shared with his majesty a plan for seizing the enemy's entire navy. The depth of the channel separating the two kingdoms, I had been assured by local seamen, was never more than seventy *glumgluffs* deep (about six feet in the European system of measurement).

I walked towards the northeast coast and,

lying down behind a hill, took out my pocket telescope. I could see the enemy's armada at anchor. It consisted of about fifty warships and a great many transport ships. Returning to my house, I ordered a great quantity of the strongest cable and bars of iron. The cable was about as thick as twine. The bars are the length and size of knitting needles. For increased strength, I tripled the cable. For the same reason, I used three iron bars at a time, twisted together. I bent the ends of the bars to create hooks.

Once I had attached fifty hooks to fifty cables, I went back to the northeast coast about a half-hour before high tide. I took off my coat, shoes, and stockings and walked into the sea wearing my leather jacket. I waded at first, and then swam in the middle for about thirty yards until I felt the bottom under my feet. I reached the enemy fleet in less than half an hour.

The sailors were so frightened when they saw me that they leaped out of their ships and swam to shore. I fastened a hook to each ship. Then I wound all the cords together. As I worked, the enemy shot several thousand arrows, many of which stuck in my hands and face. These not only hurt; they disturbed my work. I feared most for my eyes, until I took some emergency measures. One of the items I kept hidden when I was searched was a pair of glasses. I took these out and fastened them as strongly as I could on my nose.

Protected in this way, I went on boldly with my work. Many of the enemy's arrows struck against the glass of my spectacles with little effect. Having fastened all the hooks, I took the knotted cables in my hand and began to pull. The ships did not stir, held firmly by their anchors. I cut the ships loose from their anchors with my knife, receiving about two hundred arrow shots to my face and hands in the meantime. I picked up the cables again and easily hauled away fifty of the enemy's largest warships.

The Blefuscudians, who had no idea what I intended, were astonished. They had seen me cut the cables and thought I'd simply let the ships run adrift. When the entire fleet started moving away, they began to scream in a way I cannot describe. Once out of danger, I stopped awhile to pick the arrows out of my hands and face. I rubbed on some of the ointment I had been given when I first arrived in Lilliput. I took off my glasses and waited for the tide to fall a bit. Then I waded through the middle of the channel with my cargo, arriving safely at the royal port of Lilliput.

The emperor and his whole court stood on the shore awaiting the outcome of this great adventure. They saw the ships moving forward but could not spot me. The emperor concluded I had drowned and that the enemy's fleet was attacking. Soon enough, however, his fear eased. As the channel grew shallower, I got in shouting distance. Holding up the end of the cable, I cried in a loud voice, "Long live the mighty king of Lilliput!" This great prince received me with the highest praise, granting me the title of Nardac, the highest honor in the land.

His majesty wanted me to return and bring the rest of his enemy's ships into port. So vast is the ambition of princes that he could settle for nothing less than the complete destruction of the empire of Blefuscu and the Big-endian exiles. Once crowned monarch of the whole world, he would force the survivors to break the smaller end of their eggs. I argued against this plan for reasons of justice and policy. I protested that I would never assist in the enslavement of a free and brave people. When the matter was debated in council, the wisest ministers agreed with me.

His majesty never forgave me for openly disagreeing with his scheme. He mentioned his displeasure to the council. Those who agreed with me expressed their opinion only by keeping silent. My secret enemies could not help but make some remarks that reflected poorly on me. In time, a plot to destroy me was hatched. Even the greatest service means nothing to a king if you refuse his wishes once.

About three weeks later, a formal delegation from Blefuscu arrived with humble offers of peace. Six ambassadors, supported by at least five hundred people, made a grand entrance, reflecting the importance of their business. A treaty was negotiated. Its terms were very advantageous to our emperor. During the discussions, I intervened on behalf of Blefuscu when I could. I was able to be helpful thanks to the good name I now had, or at least appeared to have at court, as a result of my part in Lilliput's victory.

The leaders of Blefuscu learned, privately, what I had done for them. As a result, they visited me. They complimented both my courage and generosity and invited me to visit their kingdom.

Finally, they asked me to demonstrate my remarkable strength about which they had heard so much. I gladly obliged them but will not trouble the reader with the details of what I did.

After entertaining my guests for a time, I asked them to do me the honor of paying my respects to their emperor. I told them I sincerely hoped to visit him before I returned to my own country. They were very pleased.

The next time I saw our emperor, I asked permission to visit the Blefuscudian monarch. He granted my wish, though I felt a certain coldness in his answer. I learned later from a confidential source that Flimnap and Bolgolam had convinced the king my visit with Blefuscu's ambassadors was a sign of my disloyalty. For the first time, I began to understand the truth about courts and ministers.

It should be noted that Blefuscu's ambassadors spoke to me through an interpreter. The languages of the two empires are as different as the differences between any two countries in Europe. Each nation took excessive pride in the beauty and history of its native tongue. Our emperor, thanks to the advantage of victory, forced the ambassadors to conduct the entire negotiation in Lilliputian. Most of the nobles and rich folks from both countries can converse in either language. A few weeks later, I did cross the channel to pay my respects to the emperor of Blefuscu. The ability of those in Blefuscu to speak Lilliputian proved fortunate for me at a time of great personal misfortune. But that tale I shall tell later.

The reader may remember that I disliked some of the provisions of the agreement that gave me my freedom. Some of the requirements were rather humiliating. Such duties were considered below me now that I was a Nardac of the highest rank. The emperor never once mentioned them to me. However, it was not long before I had an opportunity to perform what I considered at the time, a most extraordinary service.

One night, at midnight, I was awakened by the alarmed cries of voices. No fewer than a hundred people were at my door. Stirred so suddenly from a deep sleep, I was convinced I was in terrible danger. I heard the word *burglum* repeated incessantly. At last I learned from some representatives of the emperor that the queen's apartment was on fire. Her maid, having fallen asleep while reading a romance novel, was at fault. I got up in an instant.

The way was cleared for me. A bright moon helped me get to the palace without trampling on anyone. They had already set up ladders on the walls of the apartment. There were enough buckets, as well. But water was rather far away. Their buckets were only about the size of large thimbles. Though a line of volunteers supplied water as fast as they could, the flames burned so violently it was not helping. I could have used my coat to snuff out the fire, but I had left it behind. The situation was desperate. I was convinced that everything on the palace grounds would be reduced to ashes.

Suddenly, I had a brainstorm. The evening before, I had drunk plentifully a most delicious wine called *glimigrim*. Fortunately, I had not discharged myself of any part of it. The heat of the flames and the vigorous activity of attempting to douse the flames made the wine move quickly through my system. By careful application of my urine, I extinguished the fire in minutes. The palace grounds, constructed over many years, were saved from destruction.

At daylight, I returned to my house. I did not even wait for the emperor's congratulations. I had performed a great service, but I wasn't sure how his majesty would feel about the way I had performed it. After all, it is a serious offense for anyone to make water on the palace grounds. As it turned out, I could take little comfort in the message I received from the emperor. It said he would order the Supreme Court to grant me a pardon, if possible. In addition, he noted that the empress, horrified at what I had done, had moved to the most distant end of the grounds. She declared that she would never again use her apartment. And, in the presence of her advisors, she swore revenge.

I intend to write another book describing Lilliput in detail. However, in this volume I will attempt to satisfy the curiosity of my readers with some general information. The average size of the natives is somewhat less than six inches. Their animals, as well as plants and trees, are in exact proportion. By stretching out my arm, I could just reach the tops of the trees in the great royal park. The tallest horses and oxen are between four and five inches in height, the sheep an inch and half, more or less. Smaller animals are proportionally smaller. The very smallest were almost invisible to me. But nature has adapted the eyes of the Lilliputians to their needs. They see close objects with amazing precision. I have seen a cook pulling the feathers off a lark the size of a common fly. I witnessed a young girl threading what was for me an invisible needle with invisible silk. Lilliputians do not, however, see well at any great distance.

I shall say only a little in this book about education in Lilliput. Scholarship and teaching in all branches of learning have flourished there for centuries. Their writing is very peculiar. They do not write from left to right, like the Europeans, or from right to left, like the Arabians, or up to down, like the Chinese. Instead, they write diagonally, from one corner of the paper to the other, like ladies in England.

The Lilliputians bury their dead with their heads pointed down. Their faith teaches that in eleven thousand moons the dead shall rise again. By that time, they further believe, the earth (which they think is flat) will have turned upside down. Their burial practice ensures that, at their resurrection, everyone will be ready, standing on their feet. The learned among them consider this doctrine absurd. But the practice continues among the common folk.

Some laws and customs in this empire are very peculiar. If they did not completely contradict what we do in England, I could easily explain the logic behind them. Take, for example, the way informers are treated in Lilliput. As in England, crimes against the government are severely punished. But in Lilliput, if the accused is found innocent, whoever brought the complaint is immediately put to death. The innocent man is richly rewarded as payment for damages. In addition, the emperor grants him some public honor. And his innocence is proclaimed throughout the city.

Lilliputian law regards fraud a greater crime than theft. Conviction usually means death. The citizens of Lilliput consider theft a crime you can prevent with proper care and alertness. On the other hand, a swindler can commit fraud anywhere there is buying and selling. The honest man has no defense against the sly man.

They say government turns on reward and punishment. But only in Lilliput have I seen reward actually tried. Anyone who can prove he has observed the law for seventy-three moons is richly rewarded. The inhabitants I met were horrified that only punishment is used in England. Lilliputians say Justice has six eyes: two in front, two in back, and one on each side. She is watchful. She has a sword in its sheath on her left side. In her right hand is an open bag of gold. She is better prepared to reward than to punish.

In Lilliput, a man is more likely to be hired for a government job for being moral than for being skilled. Lilliputians consider government something everyone should understand. So, honesty and self-control, along with experience and good intention, best qualify a man for service, except in cases where very specific training is required. They believe that a mistake committed in ignorance by someone with good intentions never does as much damage as what a corrupt man does on purpose.

I respect many of Lilliput's ancient laws but not some of her new customs. After all, even in Lilliput men and laws can be corrupted. It was not long ago that the grandfather of the emperor now in power started the dishonorable practices I described earlier— dancing on ropes, leaping over sticks, and creeping under them. They became important customs in a short space of time, thanks to the abuses of political parties.

Lilliputians think differently than Englishmen about the duties of parents and children. The union of male and female is based on the natural instinct for preservation of the species. Men and women, they maintain, join together on the basis of strong physical desire. The Lilliputians, therefore, do not hold that a child is under any obligation to his father or his mother for bringing him into the world. After all, with the misery human life brings, it is hardly a benefit to have been conceived. When a child is being conceived, the parents are not thinking about such benefits. They are thinking other thoughts completely in their love encounters. The Lilliputians conclude that parents should be the last people entrusted with the education of their own children. Therefore, they have public nurseries in every town. There, by law, all children—except those in the working class—are sent to be educated. Several kinds of schools have been established, all segregated by sex. The teachers are trained to help children prepare for lives like their parents. I shall describe the male nurseries and then the female.

In the nurseries for males of noble birth, learned professors and several assistants are employed. The children dress and eat simply and plainly. They learn the principles of honor, justice, courage, modesty, mercy, religion, and love of country. They keep busy all day long. The time set aside for eating and sleeping is short. Children engage in vigorous exercises two hours a day. Teacher's assistants dress them until they are four. After that age even children of royal families dress themselves. Children work and play in small and large groups, accompanied by a professor. Their parents visit only twice a year, for an hour. Parents are allowed to kiss children only when meeting and saying good-bye. A professor stands by to enforce the ban on whispering, hugging, and presents of toys or candy. Every family pays for the education of their children. The king's own officers collect overdue charges.

The nurseries for children of merchants and craftsmen are similar. Children of tradesmen, however, become apprentices at seven years old. Children from families with higher status continue their studies until fifteen. Time spent at the school becomes less in each of the last three years.

In the female nurseries, the young girls of nobles are educated like the males. Female servants dress them (though always in the presence of a professor) until they are five years old. After that age, they dress themselves. Any servant caught entertaining girls with frightening or foolish tales is publicly whipped, imprisoned for a year, and sent to the bleakest part of the country. Young ladies in Lilliput are as brave and wise as young men. They despise jewelry and make-up and value only decency and cleanliness.

There are very few differences in the education of females and males. The exercises for females are a bit less vigorous. They are taught some rules relating to homemaking. Their curriculum is more restricted. In Lilliput people say, "A wife should always be a reasonable and agreeable companion, because she cannot always be young." When girls turn twelve and are therefore of a marriageable age, their parents or guardians take them home. They thank the teachers and rarely leave without some tears from the young lady and her friends.

In the nurseries of females of lower class families, children are instructed in all kinds of activities proper for their sex. Those selected to be apprentices are dismissed at seven years old. The others stay until they are eleven.

Lower class families with children at these nurseries pay a low annual fee and a portion of their earnings. Lilliputians consider nothing more unjust than to bring children into the world and then expect the public to support them. People in the upper classes set aside a certain sum for each child. The schools manage these funds fairly and wisely.

Farmers and laborers keep their children at home. Their education is of little consequence to the public. The elderly among them are supported by hospitals. Begging is unknown in the empire.

I lived in Lilliput nine months and thirteen days. I'll take this opportunity to describe my style of life there. I designed and had built a table and chair from the largest trees in the royal park. Two hundred seamstresses were hired to make shirts and linens for my bed and table. They used the strongest cloth they could get, quilted together in several layers. The seamstresses took my measurements as I lay on the ground. One stood at my neck and another at my thigh. They extended a strong cord between them. A third seamstress measured the length of the cord with a ruler one inch long. Then they measured my right thumb. That was all they needed. They know the ratio between the size of the thumb and the wrist, neck, waist, and so on. They also used my old shirt as a guide.

Three hundred tailors were hired to make my other clothing. They measured me using another method. As I kneeled on the ground, they raised a ladder to my neck. By dropping a cord from my collar to the floor, they determined the length of my coat. I measured my waist and arms myself.

Everything had to be sewn at my house, the only indoor space large enough, When finished, my clothes looked like the patchwork quilts made by ladies in England, except my patches were all the same color.

I had three hundred cooks to prepare my food, living in convenient little huts built just outside my house. Each family would prepare two dishes. I would take twenty waiters in my hand and place them on the table. A hundred more attended below on the ground. Some held dishes of meat. Others carried barrels of wine and various liquors on their shoulders. Waiters using cleverly designed ropes drew up my drink. A dish of their meat was one mouthful. A barrel of their liquor made one reasonable swallow. Our mutton is better than theirs, but their beef is excellent. I have had a sirloin so large that I needed three bites to finish it. But that is unusual. My servants were astonished to see me consume their meat bones and all, as in our country we eat the leg of a lark. Their geese and turkeys I usually ate one to a mouthful. They are far more delicious than ours. I could fit twenty or thirty of their smaller fowl on the end of my knife.

One day his imperial majesty desired the pleasure of dining with me. He came, joined by the royal family and others. I placed chairs from the palace on my table opposite where I sit. I directed guards to stand around them. Flimnap, the lord high treasurer, also attended. He carried a white staff, the symbol of his office. I noticed he often looked at me suspiciously. I pretended not to notice and instead ate more than usual, to bring honor to England and amaze my visitors. I have reason to believe that his majesty's visit gave Flimnap the opportunity to criticize me to his master. Outwardly, Flimnap always treated me favorably. But such behavior does not come easily to someone with his sour disposition. Indeed, Flimnap had always been my secret enemy. He would remind the emperor that his treasury was getting low, that they were forced to borrow money to support me. He claimed I had cost his majesty more than a million and a half *sprugs*. (Their greatest gold coin, about the size of a sequin.) He advised the emperor to dismiss me as soon as possible.

At this point, I must rescue the reputation of an excellent lady who suffered innocently on my account. The treasurer got it in his head to be jealous of his wife. Someone spread some malicious gossip that this lovely lady had become overly attached to me. It was even rumored that she had once come to my lodging secretly. This I solemnly declare to be a most wicked lie, with no basis in truth. I admit she often came to my house but never in private. She always came with at least three chaperones, usually her sister and young daughter and a friend. My servants will testify that they never saw a carriage at my door without knowing who had arrived. I defy the treasurer and his two spies (I will name them, and hope this revelation gets back to Lilliput), Clustril and Drunlo, to prove that anyone ever came to me undercover except the secretary Reldresal, who was sent by his imperial majesty. I would not have devoted so much space to this story if it hadn't involved the reputation of a great lady. This thoughtless gossip caused the treasurer to think ill of his wife for some time. And whatever he thought of her, he thought much worse of me. Suddenly, I found my standing with the emperor himself falling because the treasurer had a lot of influence with him.

PART I
Chapter 7

To understand the story of my departure from Lilliput, the reader must know about the secret plot against me at the royal court.

In England I was not a member of the upper classes and, therefore, I was a total stranger to court life. I had heard and read about the devious nature of great princes and ministers but never expected to learn about it firsthand, especially in some distant country. I never thought I would personally feel the terrible effects of court intrigues in a country governed (or so I believed) by higher principles than the courts of Europe.

The story begins as I was preparing to pay my respects to the emperor of Blefuscu. An important member of the royal court came to visit me privately, under cover of darkness. I had been of some assistance to this gentleman when he fell out of favor with his majesty. He arrived in a sedan chair carried by two servants. I dismissed the guards who usually watched over my royal guests. I put the sedan chair, with his lordship in it, into my coat pocket. I told a trusty servant to tell anyone who might ask that I had gone to sleep. I locked the door, placed the chair on the table, and sat down next to it. We greeted one another politely. I noticed then that his lordship's face was full of concern. He asked me to hear him out patiently in an important matter concerning my honor and my life.

I took notes as he related the following:

"You should know that several committees have met in secret recently to discuss you. Two days ago, his majesty arrived at a decision.

"You are well aware that Skyresh Bolgolam has been your deadly enemy from the moment you arrived. I do not know his original reasons. I do know his hatred has increased since your great success against Blefuscu. Your achievement dimmed his glory as high-admiral. Working with Flimnap the high-treasurer (whose hatred of you on account of his wife is well known) and others, Skyresh Bolgolam has prepared official articles of treason against you."

I wanted so much to plead my innocence that I was going to interrupt him. He requested my silence and went on: "Out of gratitude for the favors you have done me, I obtained a copy of the accusations."

I present the text here for my readers:

Articles of Treason Against **QUINBUS FLESTRIN** (the Man-Mountain)

ARTICLE I.

An ancient law declares that urinating within the grounds of the royal palace is a crime of treason. Nevertheless, the accused openly defied the law under the pretense of extinguishing the fire in the apartment of his majesty's most dear wife.

ARTICLE II.

The aforementioned Quinbus Flestrin, after bringing the imperial fleet of Blefuscu into the royal port, refused the command of his imperial majesty to seize the remaining ships of Blefuscu. Such a complete victory would have enabled us to put to death all the Big-endian exiles and end—once and for all—this Big-endian blasphemy. Instead, this traitor claimed to be unwilling to destroy the liberties and lives of an innocent people.

ARTICLE III.

When ambassadors arrived from the Court of Blefuscu to sue for peace in his majesty's court, the said Flestrin, did, like a traitor, entertain the said ambassadors although he knew they served an enemy of his imperial majesty.

ARTICLE IV.

Even now, the accused is preparing to travel to the court of Blefuscu with nothing more than verbal permission from his imperial majesty. Under cover of that permission, he intends to aid and abet our enemy, the emperor of Blefuscu.

His lordship continued, "There are some other articles, but these are the most important. I must tell you that during the debates over these accusations, his majesty often reminded the committee of the services you have performed. The treasurer and admiral insisted that you should be sentenced to a painful death. Your house would be set on fire. As you attempted to escape, twenty thousand men armed with poisoned arrows would shoot your face and hands. Some of your servants were to be secretly ordered to soak your shirts and sheets in a poison so powerful you would try to tear off your flesh. You would die in agony. The lord high general agreed as well. The majority was against you. At the last moment, however, his majesty decided your life should be spared. He was able to convince one of the ministers as well.

"At this point, Reldresal, principal secretary for private affairs, who always considered himself your true friend, was asked his opinion by the emperor. His remarks proved his loyalty. He recognized the serious nature of your crimes but insisted there was room for mercy from our worthy king. Reldresal admitted that some might think him partial due to your well-known friendship. He reminded everyone that the king had commanded him to respond. He proposed that his majesty spare your life in return for the services you have rendered. Instead, he suggested that if both of your eyes would be put out, the world would applaud the emperor's compassion. Without eyes you might still be useful to his majesty. Blindness, he continued, adds to courage by concealing danger. In the future, you would see only through the eyes of ministers, as all great leaders do.

"This proposal angered the entire board. Bolgolam, the admiral, lost his temper completely. He demanded to know how Reldresal could presume to spare the life of a traitor. The same characteristics that allowed you to perform all of your so-called services could be turned against Lilliput. A stream of urine that doused a fire could flood the whole palace. The strength that seized the Blefuscu fleet could return it. And, most seriously of all, he had good reason to think you were a Big Endian at heart. And, since treason begins in the heart, he condemned you as a traitor for that reason alone. He then insisted you be put to death.

"The treasurer agreed. He showed how your upkeep was draining his majesty's treasury. Putting out your eyes would, most likely, increase expenses. He reminded the board of the common practice of blinding some kinds of fowls. Their movements decrease, their feeding increases, and they grow fat sooner. In conclusion, he added, your guilt is so firm in the minds of everyone in the council that the formal proofs required by law are unnecessary. We should condemn you to death immediately.

"But his imperial majesty remained firm against capital punishment. If taking your eyes is too lenient, he said, then an additional punishment should be administered afterwards. Your supporter, Reldresal, suggested gradually reducing your food allotment. Doing so would answer the treasurer's concerns about the treasury. As for you, you would lose weight, grow weak, and eventually die. Your carcass would be less of a problem because of your reduced size. Immediately after you died, five or six thousand of his majesty's subjects could cut your flesh from your bones and cart it away in two or three days. Your skeleton would remain, a monument for future generations to admire.

"Thanks to the secretary's suggestion, the matter was settled. The sentence of putting out your eyes was entered on the books. The project of starving you by degrees was to be kept secret. Only Bolgolam objected. As the queen's strongest supporter, he had no choice. She bears eternal hatred to you for the notorious and illegal method you used to put out the fire in her apartment.

"In three days, your friend the secretary will come to your house. He will read the articles against you. He will announce the punishment:

the loss of your eyes. You will submit (or so the emperor believes), grateful for the leniency of his majesty and his council. Twenty of his majesty's surgeons will make sure the operation is properly done. You will lie on the ground. Archers will shoot arrows with very sharp points into your eyes.

"You must decide for yourself what to do. I must immediately return as secretly as I came."

His lordship left me, with my mind full of doubt.

I did not understand all this talk of leniency. I regarded my punishment as quite harsh. I considered appealing my sentence. Though I could not deny the facts, I was sure I could prove there had been extenuating circumstances. However, after all of the trials I have observed, I have learned the truth. Every trial ends the way the judge wants it to end. I would not risk my life on the whims of any judge.

I considered resisting. No force in the empire was strong enough to subdue me. I could easily destroy the capital city. But I rejected that idea. I remembered the oath I had sworn to the emperor, the favors I had received from him, and the high title of Nardac he conferred upon me. Despite the severity of my sentence, I was not one of those members of a royal court who forgets his obligations.

Some might criticize my final decision. But thanks to my rashness, I have my eyes and my liberty. I already had his imperial majesty's permission to call on the emperor of Blefuscu. Now I only had three days to act. I sent a letter to my friend the secretary. I told him of my intention to go to Blefuscu, in keeping with the permission the king had granted me. Without waiting for a response, I went to the side of the island where our fleet lay. I seized a large warship, tied a cable to its end, and lifted up its anchors. I removed my clothes and used the vessel to store them. Sometimes wading and sometimes swimming, I reached the royal port of Blefuscu. There, the people had long expected my arrival. Two guides directed me to the capital city. When I got there, I sent the guides to announce my appearance. In about an hour, his majesty, attended by the royal family and great officers of the court, was coming out to receive me. I stepped forward a hundred yards. No one was afraid to approach. I lay on the ground to kiss the hands of his majesty and the empress. I told his majesty, "I have kept my promise, with the permission of the emperor my master. I am honored to see you, a mighty monarch. I freely offer any service I can perform that is in keeping with my duty to my own prince." I did not mention my disgrace. Since I had not yet been informed through proper channels, I could pretend ignorance in the matter. I also had no reason to believe the emperor of Lilliput would discover I knew what he had planned for me. However, I was wrong.

I shall not bother telling the reader how I was welcomed at the court of Blefuscu. I will say it was a reception that one might expect from so great a prince. I also will not mention the problems I had in lacking a home and a bed. I was forced to sleep on the ground wrapped in my own coat.

PART I
Chapter 8

Three days after my arrival, I took a walk to the northeast coast of the island. I noticed a mile or two offshore something that looked like an over-turned boat. I took off my shoes and stockings and waded out two or three hundred yards. The tide kept bringing the object closer. Soon, I could plainly see it was a full-sized boat, most likely driven from a ship by a storm. I returned immediately to the city. I asked his imperial majesty to lend me twenty of the tallest vessels he had left and three thousand seamen, under the command of his vice-admiral. As the fleet sailed around, I returned overland to the coast, where I first discovered the boat.

The tide had driven it still nearer. The seamen were given rope, strands of cord I had twisted together for added strength. When the ships arrived I waded to within a hundred yards of the boat. Then I swam the rest of the way. The seamen threw me the end of the cord, which I fastened to a hole in the front of the boat. I tied the other end to a warship. However, I found the sea too deep at this point to do what I intended. Instead, I was forced to swim behind and push the boat forward as often as I could, with one of my hands. Luckily, the tide was in my favor. Soon, I had gotten far enough that I could just touch the bottom while keeping my chin above water. I rested two or three minutes and then gave the boat another shove. When the sea was no higher than my armpits, the hardest part was over. I took out other cables, which I had stored in one of the ships. I fastened them first to the boat and then to nine of the Blefuscu ships. With a favorable wind, the seamen were able to tow the boat within forty yards of the shore. At low tide I was able to reach the boat without getting wet. With the assistance of two thousand men, I turn the boat on its bottom and found it was only slightly damaged.

Once I had made some paddles—which took me ten days—I was able, with some difficulty, to get my boat to the royal port of Blefuscu. There thousands greeted my arrival. They were astonished at the sight of such a huge boat. I told the emperor good fortune had thrown this boat my way so I could return to my homeland. I begged his majesty's assistance in getting together the necessary materials and permitting my departure. After some kind words, he granted my wishes.

I wondered why, in all this time, no important communications about me had come from my emperor to the court of Blefuscu. I learned later that his imperial majesty never realized what I had in mind. He believed I had only gone to Blefuscu as promised and in accordance with the permission he had granted. He was confident I would return in a few days. Finally, he became curious about my long absence. After consulting with the treasurer and the rest of that bunch, a trustworthy messenger was sent to deliver a copy of the articles against me. He presented them to the monarch of Blefuscu, pointing out the great mercy of his master, who was content to punish me no farther than with the loss of my eyes. He made it clear to the king that I had fled from justice. If I did not return in two hours, I would be deprived of my title of Nardac, as well as my eyes, and declared a traitor. The king's representative added that in order to maintain the peace between both empires, his master expected the emperor of Blefuscu to cooperate. He should give orders to have me sent back to Lilliput immediately, bound hand and foot, to be punished as a traitor.

The emperor of Blefuscu consulted with his ministers for three days. His reply was full of courtesy and excuses. He reminded the emperor of Lilliput that it would be impossible to return me tied up. Furthermore, although I had deprived him of his fleet, he owed me much for services I had performed during the peacemaking. Most importantly, the problem would soon be solved. In a few weeks, both empires would be freed of this burden. A large boat had been found that would carry me out to sea. The emperor himself had given orders to help make the vessel seaworthy under my direction.

With this answer, the envoy returned to Lilliput. The monarch of Blefuscu told me everything. In the strictest confidence, he offered me his protection. In return, I would continue in his service. I had already promised myself to never again trust any kings or ministers. Therefore, I thanked him and humbly begged to be excused. I told him that since fortune, whether good or evil, had thrown a vessel in my way, I had decided to venture out into the ocean. No longer would I be a cause of friction between two such mighty monarchs. The emperor was not at all displeased. In fact, I learned later that he greatly approved of my decision.

As a result of my concern about monarchs and ministers, I decided to move along more quickly. I would depart even sooner than I intended. Blefuscu's emperor, all too happy to be rid of me, was glad to contribute. Five hundred workmen made two sails for my boat according to my specifications. I painstakingly made satisfactory ropes and cables by twisting together a many as thirty of the thickest and strongest of theirs. A great stone that I happened to find became my anchor. The tallow of three hundred cows proved sufficient for greasing my boat and other uses. I carefully selected the largest timber for oars and masts. His majesty's ship-carpenters helped me smooth them after I had done the rough work.

In about a month, I was ready. I sent word to his majesty. I awaited only his command before leaving. The emperor and royal family came out of the palace. I lay down on my face to kiss his hand, which he very graciously gave me. So did the empress and royal princes. His majesty presented me with fifty purses of two hundred *sprugs* apiece, together with a full-length portrait. I immediately put it into one of my gloves, to keep it from being hurt. The ceremonies at my departure were too extensive to describe here.

I supplied the boat with sides of meat from a hundred oxen and three hundred sheep. I took generous supplies of bread and drink as well. For immediate use, I took as much sliced meat as four hundred cooks could provide. I took six live cows and two bulls and as many ewes and rams. I hoped to establish herds in my own country. To feed them, I had a sizeable bundle of hay and a bag of corn. I would gladly have taken a dozen of the natives, but the emperor would not permit me. My pockets were searched and I pledged not to "carry away any of your subjects, even if they want me to do so."

I set sail on the twenty-fourth day of September 1701, at six in the morning. The wind was from the southeast. When I had gone about ten miles northward, I spotted a small island. There I cast anchor, out of the wind. Seeing no sign of inhabitants, I ate and rested. I slept for at least six hours. It was a clear night. Day broke two hours after I awoke. I ate my breakfast before the sun came up. As the wind was favorable, I got an early start, steering in the same direction as the day before. My pocket compass proved quite valuable. Based on my belief that I was in the vicinity of Tasmania, I intended to reach one of the islands to the northeast. I did not sight land the next day. By the middle of the following day I estimated I was more than two hundred miles from Blefuscu. At about three in the afternoon, I spied a sail to the southeast. I headed due east. I hailed her. I could get no answer, but I was gaining on her. In half an hour she spied me. A flag was hung out and a signal gun fired.

How can I express my joy? I could now hope I might once more see my beloved country and my dear children. I pulled up to the ship between five and six in the evening, on September 26th. As I got closer my heart leaped to see her flying the English flag. I put my cows and sheep into my coat pockets, and got on board with my cargo. The vessel

was an English merchant ship returning from
Japan. The captain was Mr. John Biddel, a very
courteous man and an excellent sailor.

We had met up at a latitude of 30 degrees
south. There were about fifty men in the ship. I
even chance upon an old friend, Peter Williams,
who confirmed my good impression of the captain. This gentleman treated me with kindness. He
asked me to tell where I came from and where I
was heading. I did so, very briefly. He thought I
was raving mad, that the dangers I had faced had
disturbed my head. I took the cattle and sheep out
of my pocket. Now he was convinced I was telling
the truth. I showed him the gold the emperor of
Blefuscu had given me. I also took out his
majesty's full-length portrait and some other
unusual souvenirs. I gave him two purses of two
hundred *sprugs* each. I also promised that he could
have a cow and pregnant sheep when we reached
England. Thanks to his biscuits, which I ground
into powder, my livestock were able to survive on
board the ship.

I need say no more about this voyage other
than that it was very successful for the most part.
We arrived in England on the 13th of April, 1702.
I had only one misfortune. Rats on board the ship
carried away one of my sheep. I found her bones
in a hole, picked clean from the flesh. The rest of
my livestock I got safely ashore. I put them out to
graze in a lawn grown for bowling. The fine grass

there they ate heartily. In the short time I spent in England, I made a tidy profit by exhibiting my cattle for a fee. Before I began my next voyage, I sold them for six hundred pounds. When I returned, the breed had increased, especially the sheep. I hope their fine wool will be good for the wool industry.

Once home, I stayed only two months with my wife and family. I still had an insatiable desire to see foreign countries. I left a large sum of money with my wife and set her up in a good house. In an attempt to make some money, I took the rest of my savings with me, in goods as well as cash. My elderly uncle, John, had left me some land that rented for about thirty pounds a year. That was enough to support the family in my absence. My son Johnny, named after his uncle, was a promising child. My daughter Betty (who is now married with children) was then working as a seamstress. I said goodbye to my wife and boy and girl. Everyone cried as I left to board the *Adventure*, a merchant ship. My account of that voyage will be described in the Second Part of my Travels.

GULLIVER'S TRAVELS

PART II

A Voyage to Brobdingnag

PART II
Chapter 1

I shipped out on the 20th day of June, 1702, on the *Adventure*. We had favorable winds until we reached the Cape of Good Hope. Landing to re-supply our fresh water, we discovered a leak. We unloaded our cargo and wintered there. The captain fell sick and we were unable to leave the Cape until the end of March.

We had a good voyage until we passed the Straits of Madagascar. There, the prevailing wind blows north to west from December to May. On April 19th it began to blow more violently, and more from the west than usual. It continued for about twenty days. On May 2nd the wind ceased. There was perfect calm. I rejoiced, but the captain knew better. He warned the crew to prepare for a storm. The next day, the southern monsoon began.

Knowing the wind would be strong, we had taken every necessary precaution. It was a very fierce storm, but the ship and crew held up bravely. When the storm was over, we re-set the sails and headed into the wind.

By my computation, the storm had driven us as much as fifteen hundred miles to the east. Not even the oldest sailor on board could tell where we were. Our food supplies were holding out well. The ship was sound. The crew was all in good health. But we desperately needed water. We decided to continue in the same direction rather than heading north. Siberia and the Frozen Sea lay somewhere in that direction.

On the 16th day of June, 1703, we spotted land. On the 17th, we came in full view of a great island or continent (we didn't know which). On the south side was a small neck of land jutting out into the sea. There a shallow creek emptied. We cast anchor within a few miles of this creek. The captain sent a dozen well-armed men in the longboat to collect water. I asked to go with them, curious to see the country and make any discoveries I could. On landing, we saw no river or spring and no sign of inhabitants. Our men wandered along the shore to find fresh water. I walked alone about a mile in the other direction. I began to get tired and started returning slowly to the boat. To my surprise, the men had already boarded. They were rowing for dear life back to the ship. I was going to holler until I noticed a huge creature walking after them as fast as he could. The sea was barely up to his knees. He took immense strides. Fortunately, our men had a significant head start. The ocean bottom was full of sharp-pointed rocks and the monster was not able to overtake them. I learned this later, for I dared not stay to see the outcome. Instead, I ran away as fast as I could. I climbed a steep hill to get a better view. I found the land widely farmed. What surprised me most was the size of the grass. The hay was about twenty feet high.

I chanced onto what I thought was a main road. Later I learned it was only a footpath through a field. I walked on for some time. I could see very little on either side, as the corn was at least forty feet. It took me an hour to walk to the end of the field, at a hedge at least one hundred and twenty feet high. The trees were so tall I could not even estimate their height.

I found a set of steps to allow passage from this field to the next. A stone on which to cross over was set at the top. It was impossible for me to climb. Every step was six-feet high. The stone was twenty feet high. I was trying to find some gap in the hedge when I discovered one of the inhabitants in the next field. He was about the same size as the giant I had seen chasing our boat. As tall as a church steeple, he covered ten yards with every stride, as near as I could guess.

Struck with fear and astonishment, I hid in the corn. From there I saw him at the top of the steps, looking into the next field. He called in a voice so loud and from so high in the air, that at first I thought it was thunder. Seven monsters like himself came towards him with reaping hooks in their hands. These people were not as well dressed as the first giant. I assumed they were his field hands. He uttered some words and they went right to work, reaping corn in the field where I lay.

I kept as far from them as possible. Movement was difficult, however. The corn stalks were often less than a foot apart. I could hardly squeeze between them. I tried my best to keep ahead of the workers but then I got to a part of the field where the corn had been knocked down by the rain and wind. There, it was almost impossible for me to move. The stalks had fallen over one another. I could not even crawl through. The silk of the fallen ears was so thick and pointed it pierced through my clothes into my flesh. I could hear the reapers less than a hundred yards behind me.

Overcome by exhaustion and despair, I lay down between two rows. There I knew—I even hoped—my life would end. I wept for my widow and fatherless children. I regretted my foolishness in attempting a second voyage against the advice of friends and relatives. In this terrible state of mind, I could not help thinking of Lilliput, where the inhabitants looked at me as the greatest giant ever. There I hauled off an entire fleet with my bare hands. I performed feats authors will include in their history books. I felt as tiny and insignificant here as a Lilliputian would among us.

I was convinced such worries would be the least of my misfortunes. Many Englishmen believe humans are more savage and cruel the larger they are. I expected to end up a morsel in the mouth of the first of these enormous brutes who chanced to spy me. The philosophers are right when they tell us that things are great or little only in comparison to one another. I don't doubt that the Lilliputians may one day find people as small compared to them as they were to me. And who knows? In some distant part of the world may live a race of giants much taller than those I had just encountered.

Scared as I was, I could not stop my mind from racing. Suddenly, one of the reapers approached within ten yards. On his next step, I would be squashed to death under his foot or cut in two by his reaping hook. Therefore, when he started to move again, I screamed as loud as fear would allow.

The huge creature stopped short. Looking around for some time, he spotted me at last. He thought a while, as if considering how to pick up a small but dangerous animal without risking a scratch or a bite. I have done the same with a weasel. At last, he grabbed me from behind and held me between his forefinger and thumb. He

lifted me to within three yards of his eyes to see me more clearly. He pinched my sides, afraid I might slip through his fingers. Though he held me in the air more than sixty feet from the ground, I had the presence of mind not to struggle. All I did was raise my eyes towards the sun and put my hands together as if asking for something. I spoke some words in a humble tone of voice. I was afraid he might hurl me to the ground at any moment. Instead, he appeared pleased with my voice and gestures. He looked me over, amazed to hear words—even if he could not understand them—

coming from such a curious creature. In the meantime, I could not help groaning and shedding tears. I let him know, as best I could, how much the pressure of his thumb and finger hurt. He seemed to understand. Lifting up a flap on his coat, he put me gently into a pocket and ran to his master.

The farmer—the same person I had first seen—heard out his servant. Then, he took a piece of a small straw, about the size of a walking stick, and used it to touch my coat. I gathered he thought my coat might be the covering that nature had given me. He blew my hair aside to take a better view of my face. He called all of his workers and asked them (I later learned) whether they had ever seen any other creatures resembling me. He then placed me softly on the ground on all fours. I got up immediately and walked slowly backward and forward to show I had no intention of running away.

They all sat down in a circle, the better to watch what I did. I pulled off my hat and made a low bow towards the farmer. I fell on my knees, lifted up my hands and eyes, and spoke several words as loudly as I could. I took a coin purse out of my pocket and politely placed it on the palm of his hand. He drew it close to one eye to inspect it more carefully but could not understand its purpose. I made a sign to indicate he should place his hand on the ground. I opened the purse and poured all the gold into his palm. He wet the tip of his little finger with his tongue and used it to pick up one piece after another. He had no idea what they were. He made me a sign that I should put them back into my purse and the purse into my pocket. Instead, I offered the purse to him several times. When he refused, I thought it best to do as he wished.

Convinced at last that I was an intelligent creature, the farmer made many attempts to communicate. I could tell he was speaking meaningfully, though his voice was piercing to my ears. I could understand nothing but replied as loudly as I could in several languages. He placed an ear within two yards of me, but it was no use. We made no sense to each other.

He sent his servants back to work. He took out a handkerchief and spread it out on his left hand. Placing his palm flat on the ground, he made a sign for me to step into it. I obeyed. I lay full length across the handkerchief. He wrapped me up in it and, in this way, carried me safely to his house. He called his wife and showed me to her. She screamed and drew back like women in England do at the sight of a spider. However, when she saw how well I could understand the signs her husband made, her fear decreased. Eventually, she grew fond of me.

A servant brought lunch. It was a suitable meal for a farmer, one substantial plateful of meat served in a dish about twenty-four feet in diameter. Joining the farmer and his wife were three children and an old grandmother. After they sat down, the farmer placed me close to him on a table thirty feet high. I was terribly frightened and stayed as far as I could from the edge. The wife cut a bit of meat into tiny pieces, crumbled some bread on a plate, and placed it in front of me. I bowed, took out my knife and fork, and began to eat, to the delight of the entire family. A maid filled their smallest cup, which held about two gallons. With great difficulty I lifted up the vessel in both hands. Before I drank, I toasted the lady of the house in loud but respectful English. Everyone at the table laughed so heartily I was almost deafened from the noise. Their liquor tasted like hard cider and was not unpleasant.

The master signaled that I should make my way to his plate. As I walked on the table, I stumbled over a crust of bread and fell flat on my face. Unhurt, I got up immediately. Noticing the concern of my hosts, I waved my hat (which I had held under my arm out of good manners) and said hurrah three times. But as I made my way, the youngest son, a naughty boy of about ten, grabbed me by the legs. He dangled me so high in the air that I trembled. His father snatched me back and at the same time gave him a whack on the ear that would have knocked down an entire troop of European cavalry. Then he sent the child away from the table. Afraid the boy would seek revenge, I begged him to pardon his son. The father complied, and the lad sat down again. I went over to the boy and kissed his hand. The master then took his son's hand and made him pet me gently.

In the middle of dinner, I heard a noise behind me like that of a dozen weaving machines. My mistress's favorite cat had leaped into her lap. I had heard the purring of that animal, a cat three times larger than an ox. The fierceness of this creature's face upset me completely though she was at the other end of the table, fifty feet away. I've always been told that the surest way to get a fierce animal to attack is to run away from it. And so, showing no fear, I walked up to within a half yard of the creature. She drew back as if she were more afraid of me than I of her. I had even less fear of the farmer's dogs. One, a mastiff, was the size of four elephants, and another, a greyhound, was taller but not so large.

When dinner was almost done, the nurse came in with a one-year-old in her arms. The infant spotted me and immediately began to cry. He wanted me for a plaything. The mother, who was in the habit of spoiling her youngest, brought me over to the baby. He grabbed me right away and put my head into his mouth. I roared so loudly I frightened the little one, who dropped me. I would certainly have broken my neck, if the mother had not caught me in her apron. The nurse, to quiet the babe, shook a rattle (a kind of hollow vessel filled with great stones) fastened by a cable to the child's waist. It didn't calm her, so as a last resort, she nursed the child.

No object ever disgusted me as much as the sight of that monstrous breast. I cannot think of anything with which to compare it, to give the curious reader an idea of its bulk, shape, and color. It jutted out six feet and was no less than sixteen feet around. The nipple was about half the size of my head. It was marked with so many spots, pimples, and freckles that nothing could be more nauseating. This made me think about the fair skins of our English ladies. Perhaps they only appear so beautiful to us because they are our own size. Were we to see their defects through a magnifying glass, even the smoothest and whitest skin would look rough and coarse and discolored.

In my own country, I am generally regarded as quite good-looking. A learned man and trusted friend I met in Lilliput said my face appeared smooth when he looked at me from the ground. Up close, he found my skin to be a very shocking sight. He could see great holes. The hairs of my beard were ten times thicker than the bristles of a boar. My complexion was made up of several colors, all disgusting.

On the other hand, in speaking about various ladies in the emperor's court, my Lilliputian friend used to say one had freckles, another a big mouth, and a third too large a nose. I was unable to distinguish these defects. I had to mention this to make sure the reader did not think these gentle giants were deformed. On the contrary, they are a handsome race. My master, though only a farmer, was a fine specimen of a man when seen at a height of sixty feet.

When dinner was done my master went out to work, leaving his wife to take care of me. I was very tired and ready to sleep. My mistress was aware of my exhaustion. She put me on her own bed and covered me with a clean white handkerchief larger than the mainsail of a warship.

I slept about two hours, dreaming I was at home with my wife and children. Instead, I awoke in a vast room, perhaps three hundred feet wide and two hundred high, in a bed twenty yards wide. How sad that made me!

My mistress was busy with her household affairs and had locked me in. Some natural necessities obliged me to climb down the eight yards from the bed to the floor. I could not presume to request help. Had I called out, no one would have heard me. I was too distant from the kitchen.

While I considered my options, two rats crept up the curtains. Sniffing their way, they ran back and forth along the bed. When the first one came near me, I rose in fear and drew my sword. These horrible animals boldly attacked me on two sides. One leaped up to grab hold of my collar. I slashed his belly before he could do me any harm. He fell at my feet. The second rat saw what had happened to his comrade and escaped, but not before I gave him a good wound on the back. Each rat was the size of a large dog, but much more swift and fierce. Had I taken off my sword before I fell asleep, I would have been torn to pieces and devoured. I measured the tail of the dead rat. It was two yards long.

My mistress came into the room. She noticed immediately I was covered in blood. I pointed to the dead rat, smiled, and made other signs to show I was not hurt. A maid picked up the creature with a pair of tongs and threw it out the window. My mistress was overjoyed. She put me on a table. I showed her my bloody sword. Wiping it on my lapel, I returned it to the scabbard.

I was now under even greater pressure to do two things only I could do for myself. I tried my best to make my mistress understand that I wished to be put on the floor. Once there, I was too bashful to do more than point to the door and bow several times. The good woman at last understood. Taking me up again in her hand, she walked to the garden, where she set me down. I signaled for her not to look or follow me. I hid between two leaves and answered the calls of nature.

I hope, gentle reader, you will excuse me for dwelling on such matters. To someone with a simple mind such details may appear insignificant. But

it is my hope that philosophers will use them for
the benefit of the public. For that reason, I have
taken the greatest care throughout these accounts
of my travels to tell the truth without embellish-
ment. This particular voyage made such a strong
impression on my mind that I omitted almost
nothing. While revising the text, I crossed out only
a few unimportant passages, afraid of being criticized as boring and petty, as travel writers often
are.

PART II
Chapter 2

My mistress had a nine-year old daughter, a clever child for her age. She and her mother prepared the baby's cradle for me. They put the cradle into a small drawer of a cabinet. They placed the drawer on a hanging shelf as protection from rats. This was my bed the entire time I stayed with those people. As I began to learn their language, we improved the design of the bed as I was better able to make my needs known.

This young girl was so handy that she learned very quickly how to dress and undress me. However, I always preferred to do it myself. She made me seven shirts, and some other items, from the finest cloth available (which was coarser than sackcloth). She washed my clothes frequently and with her own hands. She was also my schoolmistress, teaching me their language. When I pointed to a thing, she told me the word for it in her own tongue. In a few days I was able to ask for whatever I wanted. She was very good-natured, and less than forty feet high, being small for her age. She gave me the name Grildrig, which the family adopted, and later the whole kingdom. The word means something like the English word *mannequin*. To her, I owe my survival in that country. We never parted while I was there. I called her my Glumdalclitch, or little nurse. I cannot praise her enough for the fine care she took of me and for her affection. I heartily wish I had the power to reward her as she deserves. Instead, I fear I caused her disgrace.

It became known in the neighborhood that my master had found a strange animal. It was said to be the size of a *splacnuck* (an animal in that country about six feet long), but like a human creature in every other respect. It had learned several words, walked on two legs, was tame and gentle, would come when it was called, do whatever it was asked, and had a finer complexion than a nobleman's three-year old daughter. A farmer who lived nearby visited to find out for himself the truth of this story. I was immediately brought out and placed on a table. I walked as I was commanded and drew my sword. I inquired after his health and told him, "You are welcome!" as my little nurse had instructed me. This man, who was old and dim-sighted, put on his glasses to see me better. I simply had to laugh. His eyes looked like the full moon shining through two windows. Our people realized the cause of my glee and joined me in laughing. The old fellow foolishly became angry.

My master's friend was preoccupied with money. Unfortunately, he suggested my master exhibit me (for a fee) on market day in a town twenty-two miles away, about half an hour's ride. I suspected mischief when I saw my master and his friend whispering and pointing at me. I feared the worst after I convinced myself I'd overheard and understood their words. The next morning Glumdalclitch, my little nurse, told me the whole story, which she had cleverly learned from her mother. The poor girl wept with shame and grief. She feared some rude folks would do some mischief to me. Anyone could so easily squeeze me to death or break one of my bones simply by picking me up. She knew how embarrassed I would feel as a public spectacle. She said her papa and mamma had promised I would be hers. She felt as she had a year ago when her parents pretended to give her a lamb and then sold it to a butcher as soon as it was fat.

I may truly state that I was less concerned than my nurse. I still believed I would regain my freedom one day. Furthermore, I regarded myself as a perfect stranger in this country. There was no danger that I would ever be criticized in England for being displayed as a freak of nature here. The king of Great Britain himself, in my situation, would have been treated exactly the same.

And so, on market day my master carried me in a box to the neighboring town. He took along his little daughter. The box had a little door and a few holes to let in air. It had no windows. The girl lined the floor with the quilt of her baby's bed so I could lie down. However, though the journey was only half an hour, I was terribly shaken. The horse took steps about forty feet long. His trotting felt like the rising and falling of a ship in a great storm, but much more frequent. My master stopped at one of his favorite taverns, the Green Eagle. He hired a town crier to announce the arrival of a strange creature to be seen at the Green Eagle. This creature, smaller than a *splacnuck* yet like a human creature in every way, could speak several words and entertain.

I was placed on a table in the largest room of the inn. My little nurse stood on a low stool close to the table to take care of me and tell me what to do. My master allowed in only thirty people at a time. I walked around the table as the girl commanded. Knowing exactly how much of their language I understood, she asked me questions. I answered them as loudly as I could. I turned to the audience, paid my respects, and said, "You are welcome!" I raised a thimble filled with liquor and drank to their health. I drew my sword and imitated fencers in

England. That day, I performed for twelve sets of spectators. I had to perform the same silly tricks over and over until I was half dead with exhaustion. Those who had seen me were so enthusiastic that people were ready to break down the doors to get in. My master would not allow anyone to touch me except my nurse. As a further precaution, benches were set around the table to put me out of everybody's reach. That was fine until an ill-behaved schoolboy aimed a hazelnut at my head. It was about as large as a small pumpkin and thrown so powerfully it could have knocked my brains out. Fortunately, it just missed. And I had the satisfaction of seeing the young rogue beaten and ejected.

My master gave public notice that he would show me again the next market day. In the meantime, he built a more convenient container for me. The first journey had tired me out so much (along with entertaining for eight hours) that I could hardly stand or speak a word. It took at least three days to recover my strength.

There was no rest for me at home. Everyone within a hundred miles heard of my fame and came to see me at my master's house. Usually there were at least thirty men in the audience with their wives and children. So, I had little rest all week (except Wednesday, which is their Sabbath) even when I was not carried to town.

My master, realizing how much I was worth,

decided to carry me to the most populated and important cities of the kingdom. Equipped for a long journey, he said goodbye to his wife. On the 17th of August, 1703, about two months after my arrival, we set out for the grand city located near the middle of that empire, about three thousand miles from our house. My master made his daughter Glumdalclitch ride behind him. She carried me on her lap, in a box tied around her waist. She had lined it on all sides with the softest cloth, furnished it with her baby's bed, and made everything as convenient as she could. We had no other company except a servant boy, who rode after us with the luggage.

My master's idea was to show me in all the towns along the way. He would also take side trips to towns within a hundred miles of the road, whenever it promised to be worthwhile. Each day's journey was short, no more than about 150 miles. Otherwise, to make it easier for me, Glumdalclitch would complain she was tired from all the trotting.

She often took me out of my box, at my request, to give me air and show me the country. She kept me secure with a string tied around my waist. We crossed five or six rivers, many times wider and deeper than the Nile or the Ganges. Almost every creek was bigger than the Thames at London Bridge. The journey lasted ten weeks. I was shown in eighteen large towns and many villages, as well as to private families.

On the 26th day of October we arrived at the capital, Lorbrulgrud, meaning *Pride of the Universe*. My master rented a room on the main street of the city, not far from the royal palace. He posted the usual advertisements, containing an exact description of my person and parts. He hired a large room between three and four hundred feet wide. He provided a table sixty feet in diameter on which I was to perform. Three feet from the edge he constructed a fence to prevent me from falling over. I was shown ten times a day, to the wonderment of all.

I could now speak the language fairly well and understood nearly every word. I had learned their alphabet and could read and translate their written language. Glumdalclitch continued teaching me at home and during our leisure time as we traveled. She carried a little book in her pocket about the size of our largest books. Written for young girls, it gave a short account of their religion. With this book, she taught me to read their language.

PART II
Chapter 3

All of my hard work began to affect my health. The more money my master earned, the greedier he grew. I lost my appetite and was almost reduced to a skeleton. The farmer noticed my condition. Figuring I would die soon, he decided to get whatever he could out of me. Just then a messenger came from the royal court requesting my master bring me immediately to entertain the queen and her ladies. Some of them had already seen me, and reported strange things about my beauty, behavior, and intelligence.

Her majesty and those who attended her were absolutely delighted with my manners. I fell on my knees and begged the honor of kissing her imperial foot. Instead, this gracious princess—once I had been placed on a table—held out her little finger towards me. I embraced it in both arms and put the tip of it—with the utmost respect—to my lips.

She asked me some general questions about my country and my travels, which I answered as best I could. She asked, "Could you be content living at court?"

I bowed low and humbly answered, "I am my master's slave. But if I could choose, I would proudly devote my life to her majesty's service." She then asked my master whether he was willing to sell me. Sure I would not live a month, he was ready to part with me … for a price. He demanded a thousand pieces of gold, which were delivered on the spot. Each piece was about the size of eight hundred of our coins. But considering the relative size of everything else in that country and Europe, as well as the price of gold in Brobdingnag (so it is called), the sum paid for me amounted to very little. I then said to the queen, "Since I am now your majesty's most humble servant, I must beg one favor. Please admit into your service Glumdalclitch, who has always tended me with so much care and kindness, so she can continue to be my nurse and instructor."

Her majesty agreed and easily got the farmer's consent. He was glad to have his daughter in a favored position at court. The girl was not able to hide her joy. My late master departed, bidding me farewell, saying he had left me in good hands. I did not reply and instead bowed slightly.

The queen noticed my coldness. When the

farmer was gone she asked the reason. I boldly asked her majesty how much thanks I owed my former master simply for not dashing my brains out when he first found me. "I have more than amply paid him back. He has all the profits from showing me through half the kingdom as well as the price of my sale. The life I led with him was enough to kill an animal ten times my strength. My health has been seriously damaged entertaining crowds every hour of the day. My master gave her majesty a bargain because he thought my life was in danger. I no longer fear being mistreated, under the protection of such a great and good empress who is the delight of her subjects. I have reason to hope my late master's fears were groundless. I can already feel my spirits reviving simply because of your presence."

This was my whole speech, delivered in the style peculiar to people at that court. I used some phrases Glumdalclitch had taught me.

The queen graciously made an allowance for the defects in my ability to speak their language. She was quite surprised to find so much wit and good sense in such a tiny animal. She took me in her hand and carried me to the king in his private chambers. His majesty, a very serious prince, could not see me clearly at first. He asked the queen rather coldly, "Have you grown fond of this *splacnuck*?" For such it seems he took me to be. But this princess, who brims with intelligence and humor, put me gently on my feet on his writing desk. She commanded me to tell his majesty about myself, which I did in a few words. Glumdalclitch, who could not endure letting me out of her sight, stood outside the chamber door. Asked to enter, she confirmed my account of everything that had happened since I first appeared at her father's house.

The king, although as learned a person as any in his kingdom, believed at first I might be a machine created by some ingenious craftsmen. But when he heard my voice and found me to be intelligent, he could not conceal his astonishment. He remained unconvinced by the story of my arrival, however. He assumed Glumdalclitch and her father had dreamed up the whole thing and taught me what to say to fetch a better price. With this in mind, he put several other questions to me. Once again he received intelligent answers flawed only by my foreign accent and imperfect knowledge of the language.

Every week three great scholars were assigned to serve the king. These gentlemen were called. After carefully examining me, each formed a different opinion of my origin. They all agreed that the usual laws of nature could not explain my existence. Every species must be equipped with the means to survive. But I would not last long on my own in their world. They inspected my teeth most carefully and determined that I was a meat eater.

Yet I could not even capture a field mouse. Even if I could catch a snail or certain insects, they doubted I would live very long on such a diet.

One expert decided I must be an embryo born prematurely. But the other two disagreed. They pointed out that my limbs were perfect and finished. Furthermore, it was apparent from my beard, (the stumps of which they could plainly see through a magnifying glass) that I was not a newborn. They were sure I was not a dwarf because no human was even close to my size. The queen's favorite dwarf, the smallest man ever known in that kingdom, was nearly thirty feet high. After much debate they concluded unanimously that I was simply an exception to the rules of nature. From the time of Aristotle to the modern day, scientists have used this wonderful solution to explain anything they could not understand. In so doing, they have prevented human knowledge from advancing.

Having heard this ridiculous conclusion, I begged to say a word or two. I assured his majesty, "I came from a country with several million like me of both sexes. In my world, the animals, trees, and houses are all in proportion to one another. Therefore, I am able to defend myself and find food, just like any of his majesty's subjects might do here." I felt this would explain away the scientists' doubts. Instead, they scornfully replied that the farmer had taught me very well.

The king, who had more sense than his learned men, dismissed them and sent for the farmer. Fortunately, he had not yet left town. The king first questioned him privately. Then, after confronting him with the young girl and me, his majesty began to think that what we told him might possibly be true. He asked the queen to take special care of me. He recommended that Glumdalclitch continue to tend me because he observed the great affection we had for each other.

As a result, the king provided for Glumdalclitch a convenient apartment at court. She had her own governess to take care of her education, a maid to dress her, and two other servants. But Glumdalclitch alone took care of me.

The queen commanded her own cabinetmaker to design and build a box to serve as my bedchamber. It was modeled on the box Glumdalclitch and I had been using. The cabinetmaker was ingenious and in three weeks finished a wooden chamber sixteen feet square and twelve high with sash-windows, a door, and two closets. The ceiling could be lifted up and down on two hinges so my bed (supplied by her majesty's upholsterer) could be easily removed and replaced. Glumdalclitch aired out and re-made the bed every day. At night she would lower it into the box and lock the roof over me.

A craftsman capable of the most delicate work made two chairs (with backs and frames of ivory), two tables, and a cabinet to store my belongings. The room was quilted on all sides, as well as the floor and the ceiling. We hoped this padding would prevent any injury to me from the carelessness of anyone who carried me and from the force of a jolt from the coach. I requested a lock for my door to prevent rats and mice from entering. The locksmith, after several attempts, made the smallest lock ever seen in that country. I kept the key in my own pocket, afraid Glumdalclitch might lose it. The queen also ordered clothes to be made for me from the thinnest available silk, which was only slightly thicker than an English blanket. It was very cumbersome to wear at first. My wardrobe was in the latest fashion of the kingdom, resembling clothing designed in the Persian and Chinese styles.

The queen became so fond of my company that she insisted on dining with me. My table and chair sat on her majesty's table, just at her left elbow. Glumdalclitch stood on a stool nearby, to assist and take care of me. My silver dishes and plates, (relative to the queen's china) were no bigger than what I have seen in a London toyshop for use in a dollhouse. My little nurse kept my dishes in her pocket in a silver box, gave them to me at meals, and always cleaned them herself. The only other people allowed to dine with the queen were the two royal princesses, one sixteen and the other thirteen.

The queen had a weak stomach. Yet a modest mouthful for her was as much as a dozen English farmers could eat at one meal. For me, this was a nauseating sight for quite some time. She would crunch the wing of a lark (nine times as large as a full-grown turkey) between her teeth, bones and all. She would put a bit of bread into her mouth as big as two large loaves. She drank from a golden cup, about a barrel's worth with every sip. Her knives were twice as long as a scythe with the blade straightened. The spoons, forks, and other instruments were all in the same proportion. Glumdalclitch sometimes took me to watch tables of hungry diners using ten or a dozen of those enormous knives and forks at the same time. It was the most terrible sight I had ever seen.

Every Wednesday, the king and queen, along with the royal offspring, dine together in his majesty's private apartment. As a great favorite of the king, my little chair and table were placed at his left hand. The king enjoyed conversing with me. He was especially curious about manners, religion, laws, government, and education in Europe. I gave him the best account I could. A man of clear understanding and good judgment, the king made very wise comments about everything I said. Sometimes I went on a bit too much about my beloved country and our wars, religious disputes, and political parties. The king would take me in his right hand and, while petting me gently with the other, ask, "Which political party do you belong to, the Wigs or the Tories?" Turning to his prime minister, he remarked, "How disgraceful are our notions of self-importance, when they can be mimicked by a little insect like Gulliver. Yet, I bet these creatures have their titles and distinctions of honor. They call their little nests and burrows houses and cities. They love, they fight, they dispute, they cheat, they betray!" And so on, while I kept my righteous anger in check. I could hardly bear to hear our noble country—the center of virtue, piety, honor, and truth—treated so disrespectfully.

But I was in no position to show my resentment. When I thought about it, I was unsure there had really been any insult. Having become accustomed to seeing everything magnified, the horror and disgust I once felt were wearing off. I imagine that, if I had seen at that moment a company of English lords and ladies in their fine clothing, strutting, bowing, and ranting, I would have been tempted to laugh, too. In fact, when the queen would place me on her hand in front of a full-length mirror, the comparison was so ridiculous that I started to think I had shrunk.

Nothing angered me more than the queen's dwarf. He had been the smallest human ever in that country (less than thirty feet high). Now that he had found someone smaller, he would strut and look big as he passed by me. He usually made a smart remark about my size. My only revenge was to call him brother or challenge him to wrestle. In other words, we exchanged insults. One day at dinner, I was minding my own business. This nasty little puppet became so annoyed at something I said that he climbed up her majesty's chair, grabbed me around my middle, and dropped me into a large silver bowl of cream. Then the coward ran away as fast as he could. I fell in head first, and, if I had not been a good swimmer, I might have drowned. Glumdalclitch happened to be at the other end of the room. The queen was in such a fright she was unable to help. My little nurse ran over and saved me, though I had already swallowed a quart of cream. She put me to bed. The only damage was to my suit of clothes, which was completely ruined. The dwarf was soundly whipped and forced to drink the bowl of cream. He was never restored to favor. Instead, the queen gave him to an important lady at court. I never saw him again, to my very great satisfaction. I could not imagine what extremes his hatred might have driven him to.

Once in the past he had played a mean trick on me that both angered the queen and made her laugh. She would have dismissed him then, if I had not intervened. Her majesty had taken a marrowbone, and, after knocking out the marrow, placed it in the dish standing up. The dwarf, noticing that Glumdalclitch was away for a moment, climbed up on her stool. Squeezing my legs together, he wedged me to my waist in the marrowbone. There I was stuck for some time, looking ridiculous. It was almost a minute before anyone knew where it was, because I considered it below me to cry out. My stockings and breeches were ruined but I was otherwise unharmed. The dwarf, at my request, received only a whipping and no further punishment.

The queen frequently teased me about my fearfulness. She used to ask me, "Are all the people of your country cowards like you?" What started it was this. In summer, flies become quite a problem in the kingdom of Brobdingnag. These repulsive insects, each as big as a lark, would pester me at dinner, buzzing around my ears. They would sometimes land on my food and leave behind their disgusting feces or eggs, which were easily visible to me, though not to the natives. Sometimes a fly would land on my nose, or forehead, and sting me. Their smell was very offensive. I could easily see that sticky substance our scientists tell us enables those creatures to walk on the ceiling. I had much trouble defending myself against these detestable animals and could not keep from flinching when they came near. The dwarf used to catch them in his hand, as schoolboys do, and release them under my nose, to frighten me and entertain the queen. My remedy was to slash them with my sword as they flew by.

My dexterity in so doing was much admired.

One morning Glumdalclitch put me in my box on a windowsill to give me air. After I opened up one of my windows, I sat down to eat cake for breakfast. More than twenty wasps, attracted by the smell, came flying into the room, humming louder than bagpipes. Some of them seized my cake and carried it away. Others flew around my head and face, confusing me with their noise and putting me in the utmost terror of being stung. However, I had enough presence of mind to draw my sword and attack them in the air. I killed four of them and the rest got away. I shut the window immediately. These insects were as large as pheasants. I took out their stings. Each was an inch and a half long and as sharp as a needle. I carefully preserved them. After I returned to England, I displayed them and other curiosities in several parts of Europe. I gave three to Gresham College and kept the fourth for myself.

PART II
Chapter 4

I now intend to give the reader a short description of this country, as far as my travels there will
allow. I always stayed with the queen, and she
never went more than two thousand miles from
Lorbrulgrud, the central city. She would only
accompany the king that far when he visited the
frontier. The whole extent of this prince's kingdom is about six thousand miles in length and
from three to five in width. I must conclude,
therefore, that our geographers are in error when
they suppose that nothing but sea lies between
Japan and California. It had always been my opinion that a mass of land must lie there to counter-
balance the great continent of Asia. I readily offer
my assistance in correcting our maps by joining
this vast land to the northwest parts of America.

The kingdom is a peninsula. On the northeast

edge there is a ridge of impassable mountains. Not only are they thirty miles high, but they also have volcanoes on top. Not even the most learned scholars know what sort of people live on the other side. Perhaps the land is not inhabited.

On the other three sides of Brobdingnag lies the ocean. Yet there is not one seaport in the whole kingdom. Wherever rivers flow to the coast, the ocean is full of pointed rocks. In addition, the sea is so rough that sailing is too dangerous. As a result, the people of Brobdingnag do not trade goods with the rest of the world. On the other hand, their large rivers are full of ships and abound with excellent fish. They rarely bother catching fish from the ocean because there they are the same size as those in Europe. Now and then a whale happens to be dashed against the rocks and the common people feed on it heartily. I have personally seen whales too large for a Brobdingnag man to carry. Occasionally, whales are brought to Lorbrulgrud as curiosities. I saw one of them in a dish at the king's table. It was deemed a delicacy though I could tell the king was not fond of it. I believe its size disgusted him, although I have seen larger whales in Greenland. I gather that the huge plants and animals I observed are found only on this continent. Perhaps our scientists will someday determine the reason.

The country is populous. It contains fifty-one cities, almost a hundred walled towns, and a great number of villages. Lorbrulgrud makes a fine representative example of their cities. It is split in two equal parts, on either side of a river. It contains more than eighty thousand houses and about six hundred thousand inhabitants. It is three *glomglungs* long (about fifty-four English miles) and two and a half in width. I measured it myself using the map made expressly for the king. It was laid on the ground for me. It extended a hundred feet. I measured it with reasonable accuracy by pacing it barefoot several times.

The king's palace is no regular structure. Rather, it is a mass of buildings about seven miles around. Important rooms are generally two hundred and forty feet high, and broad and long in proportion.

Glumdalclitch and I had use of a coach. Her governess frequently took her out to see the town or to shop. I always joined them, carried in my box. She would often take me out and hold me in her hand so I could view the houses and people more conveniently. One day the governess ordered our coachman to stop at several shops. Whenever we stopped, beggars crowded around, providing the most horrible sight a European eye ever beheld. There was a woman with cancer in her breast. It was monstrously swollen and full of holes. I could easily have crept into two or three of them. There was a fellow with a cyst in his neck, larger than five bales of wool. Another had wooden legs, each about twenty feet high. Most disgusting of all were the lice crawling on their clothes. I could see the limbs of these vermin with my naked eye, more clearly than if I had viewed a European louse through a microscope. I watched as they used their noses to root on their hosts. I would have dissected one if I had my instruments. As it was, however, just the sight of them turned my stomach.

Besides the large box in which I was usually carried, the queen ordered a smaller one to be made about twelve feet square and ten high. Designed for traveling, this bedchamber was an exact square, with a window in the middle of three of its sides. Each window was protected by iron wire on the outside, to prevent accidents on long journeys. Large staples were attached to the fourth side, which had no window. Whoever carried me when on horseback would put a leather belt through the staples and around his waist. This duty was assigned only to a trustworthy servant. In this way, I could still attend the king and queen when requested, or enjoy the gardens, or pay a visit to some great lady or minister even if Glumdalclitch happened to be out of sorts. I had become known and sought after by the most important people. Their attention, however, was probably more an attempt to win favor with the king than a true interest in me.

When I grew tired of the carriage, a servant on horseback would buckle on my box and place it on a cushion in front of him. Thanks to the windows, I could view the country on three sides. In my smaller box, I had a hammock hung from the ceiling, two chairs, and a table neatly screwed to the floor to prevent it from being tossed about by the movement of the horse or carriage. Accustomed as I was to long sea-voyages, those motions, though sometimes violent, did not distress me.

Whenever I wanted to see the town, it was always in my traveling box. Glumdalclitch held me in her lap. We rode in a kind of sedan chair carried by four men and attended by two more of the queen's servants. The people, who had often heard of me, crowded around the sedan chair. The girl was agreeable. She would ask the bearers to stop and then hold me in her hand so I could be seen more easily.

I longed to see the main temple and particularly its tower, said to be the highest in the kingdom. After my nurse carried me there, I came back disappointed. Its height is less than three thousand feet. Considering the difference between the size of those people and Europeans, its height is not in proportion to that of the greatest buildings in Europe. I must admit, however, that whatever this famous tower lacks in height, it makes up for in beauty and strength. The walls are nearly a hundred feet thick, built of carved stones about forty feet square. Each side of the building is decorated with statues of gods and emperors, cut in marble, larger than life. I measured a little finger that had fallen down from one of these statues and lay unnoticed among some rubbish; it was exactly four feet and an inch in length. Glumdalclitch wrapped it up in her handkerchief and carried it home in her pocket. She kept it with all the other trinkets children of her age are fond of collecting.

The king's kitchen is a grand building about six hundred feet high. The oven is almost as wide as the great dome of St. Paul's Church. I fear readers and critics will believe I have exaggerated a bit (as travelers are often accused of doing) if I were to describe the kitchen implements, the huge pots and kettles, or the monstrous pieces of meat turning on the spit. To avoid such criticism, I am afraid I have understated the immensity of objects in Brobdingnag. If this account should ever be translated into their language, the king and his people will have reason to complain that I belittled and falsely represented their country.

A military guard of five hundred horses attends his majesty when he goes out on special occasions. These noble steeds range from fifty-four to sixty feet high. I considered the sight of his mounted guard the most splendid I had ever seen, until I witnessed his army in battle formation. I shall speak about this elsewhere.

PART II
Chapter 5

I would have been able to live happily in Brobdingnag if my size had not exposed me to ridiculous accidents and constant danger. I now offer some examples.

Glumdalclitch often carried me into the gardens of the court in my smaller box. Sometimes she would take me out and hold me in her hand or set me down to walk. Before the dwarf left the queen's service, he followed us one day into those gardens. He and I were together near some dwarf apple trees. I couldn't resist showing off a bit by engaging in some word play involving him and the trees. Shortly after that, the spiteful rascal shook the tree directly over my head. A dozen apples, each as large as a barrel, came tumbling down around my head. One of them hit me on the back and knocked me flat on my face. Fortunately, I was not seriously hurt. The dwarf was pardoned at my request, because I had provoked him.

Another day, Glumdalclitch left me on a bit of lawn while she walked with her governess. Suddenly a violent shower of hail began to fall. I was struck to the ground by the force of it. While I was down, the hailstones pounded cruelly all over the body, as if I had been pelted with tennis balls. By creeping on all fours, I was able to seek some shelter under a row of herbs. Nevertheless, I was so bruised from head to foot, I could not go out for ten days. It is no wonder I received such a thumping. Their hailstones are eighteen hundred times as large as those in Europe. I should know, having been curious enough to weigh and measure some.

An even more dangerous accident happened in the same garden. My little nurse put me in what we both considered a secure place (which I often asked her to do, so that I might be alone with my thoughts). We had left my box at home, to avoid the trouble of carrying it. While she was away, and out of earshot, the gardener's small white spaniel got into the garden by accident. The dog, catching my scent, found me and took me in his mouth. He ran straight to his master wagging his tail, and set me gently on the ground. By good fortune he had been well taught. I had been carried between his teeth without the least hurt. He did not even tear my clothes. But the poor gardener, who knew me well and had always treated me kindly, was in a terrible fright. He gently took me up in both hands and asked how I was. I was so amazed and out of breath that I could not speak. In a few minutes I came to myself, and he carried me safely back to my little nurse. She, in the meantime, had returned to the place where she left me and was in agony over my disappearance. She severely reprimanded the gardener on account of his dog. But we kept the matter a secret, afraid of the queen's anger. As for myself, I thought it would not be good for my reputation for the story to become known.

After this accident Glumdalclitch was absolutely determined never to again allow me out of her sight. Afraid she would reach such a conclusion, I had already concealed from her a number of unlucky adventures that had happened when she left me by myself. Once a hawk, hovering over the garden, swooped down at me. Had I not defended myself with my sword, he would certainly have carried me away in his talons. Another time, walking to the top of a fresh molehill, I fell up to my neck in the hole. After that I had to make up some good excuse to explain my dirty clothes. Once, lost in thought about dear old England, I hurt my knee when I stumbled over the shell of a snail.

Smaller birds did not appear to be at all afraid of me. I do not know if that should have made me feel pleased or humiliated. They would hop to within a yard of me as they searched for worms and other food, as if no creature at all were near them. A thrush once snatched a piece of cake right out of my hand. If I attempted to catch one of these birds, it would defend itself boldly and try to peck my fingers. Then it would hop back unconcerned and continue hunting for worms or snails.

Once, I crept up behind a bird resembling a sparrow, but closer to a swan in size. I took a large stick and threw it with all my strength. Thanks to a lucky toss, I knocked it down. Seizing it by the neck, I ran in triumph to my nurse. However, the bird, which had only been stunned, recovered. I held it at arm's length out of the reach of its claws. Nevertheless, I received some serious blows to my head and body from the flapping of its wings. I was soon relieved by one of our servants, who snapped the bird's neck. I had him for dinner the next day, by the queen's command.

The Ladies in Waiting at the palace often invited Glumdalclitch to their apartments and asked her to bring me along. They took great pleasure in seeing and touching me. They would often strip me naked from top to toe and lay me at full length on their bosoms. I found this disgusting because, to tell the truth, a very offensive smell came from their skin. In mentioning this, I intend no insult to such excellent ladies. I imagine that my sense of smell was more sensitive due to my size relative to theirs. I'm sure their scent was no more disagreeable to each other, than people at court are to us in England. After all, I found their natural smell more bearable than their perfumes, which made me faint. In Lilliput, a close friend took me aside, after I had exercised on a warm day, to let me know I was giving off a strong odor. I experience such problems less than most men. But his ability to smell someone my size was heightened. I must add, at this point, that the queen, my mistress, and Glumdalclitch smelled as sweet as any lady in England.

The inconsiderate way these maids of honor used me made me quite uncomfortable. They would strip and dress in my presence. The sight of their naked bodies was far from tempting. Their skin was rough and uneven, covered with blemishes of various colors. Close up, their moles were as large as serving platters, with hair hanging from them thicker than twine. And I will say nothing more about the rest of their bodies. Without a single qualm, they would relieve themselves as I watched. I've seen one lady produce more than a thousand gallons at one sitting.

The prettiest of the maids of honor was a playful girl of sixteen. She loved to put me on her so that I would be straddling one of her nipples. She had many other such tricks as well. I hope, kind reader, you will excuse me for skipping the details. Suffice it to say that I begged Glumdalclitch to invent some excuse for not seeing that young lady any more.

One day a nephew of my nurse's governess urged her to see an execution. The condemned man had murdered one of that gentleman's best friends. Glumdalclitch was persuaded to join them against her better judgment. Both she and I disliked such spectacles. But I could not resist the lure of seeing something so extraordinary.

The criminal was tied to a chair on a specially built scaffold. His head was cut off by one blow of a sword about forty feet long. The water from the great fountains at Versailles could not match the quantity and height of the blood that spewed from his veins and arteries. The head, when it fell on the scaffold floor, bounced so violently that I flinched, though I sat a half-mile away.

Once, when I was downhearted, the queen—having heard all about my sea-voyages—tried to cheer me up with talk of sails and oars. She wondered if I could handle them. I replied that, though I was always employed as a ship's doctor or surgeon, I was sometimes called upon, in a pinch, to perform the duties of a common sailor. She added that perhaps some rowing exercise would be good for my health. I answered that I could not imagine how this would be done in their country. Their smallest boat was the size of a first-rate English man of war. Any boat I could manage would never last in any of their rivers. Her majesty said if I would design a boat, her own carpenter would make it. She promised to provide a place for me to sail.

In ten days, I had a finished boat large enough for eight Europeans, equipped with all the essential rigging. The queen was so delighted that she carried it to the king immediately. He ordered a servant to put the boat—with me in it—in a container full of water. But it was too small to allow for proper management of the oars.

The queen had anticipated the problem. She had ordered the carpenter to make a wooden trough three hundred feet long, fifty wide, and eight deep. Covered with pitch to prevent leakage, it was placed on the floor, along the wall, in an outer room of the palace. It had a drain near the bottom to let out the water when it became stale. Two servants could easily fill it in half an hour. Here I used to row for my own entertainment, as well as for the queen and her ladies. Sometimes I would put up my sail. I would steer while the ladies used their fans to provide the wind. When they grew tired, some of their servants would blow my sail forward with their breath. When I was done, Glumdalclitch would hang my boat on a nail to dry.

Once, after my boat had been placed in the trough, Glumdalclitch's governess insisted on putting me into the boat. Suddenly, I slipped through her fingers. Only the luckiest accident prevented me from falling forty feet to my death. The head of a large pin worn by the governess got caught between my shirt and the waistband of my pants. I hung suspended in the air until Glumdalclitch came to my relief.

Another time, one of the servants carelessly let a huge frog slip into the trough. As soon as my boat was placed in the water, the frog tried to climb in. The boat threatened to capsize because the weight of the frog caused it to lean. I had to throw all my weight on the other side of the boat to keep it balanced. The frog managed to get in. It immediately hopped half the length of the boat and then back and forth over my head. My face and clothes were covered with its repulsive slime. At that size, a frog is the most deformed animal you can imagine. Nevertheless, I asked Glumdalclitch to let me deal with it alone. I hit it repeatedly with one of my oars and forced it out of the boat.

The greatest danger I ever underwent in that kingdom was from a pet monkey. Glumdalclitch had locked me in her apartment while she went somewhere on business. Since the weather was warm, the window of the apartment and the windows and doors of my large box were all left open. As I sat at my table, I heard something enter the apartment and move about rapidly. Though I was scared, I dared to look out. I saw this playful animal jumping around. He noticed my box and was quite curious about it. He looked in the door and windows. I ran to the most distant corner of my room. The sight of that monkey looking in frightened me so much that I didn't have the presence of mind to hide under the bed. The chattering monkey spotted me at last. He reached in the door with one of his paws, like a cat playing with a mouse. Even though I moved constantly, he was finally able to grasp the lapel of my coat and drag me out. He grabbed me with his right front foot and held me as a nursing mother would. I have seen monkeys do the same with a kitten in Europe. When I attempted to struggle he squeezed me so hard I decided it was more practical to submit. He stroked my face gently with his other paw. He probably mistook me for a young male of his species.

He was interrupted suddenly by the sound of someone opening the door. He leaped up to the window through which he had entered. From there he climbed up the gutters, walking on three legs, while holding me in the fourth. In this way, he reached the roof next to ours. I heard Glumdalclitch give a shriek as he was carrying me out. The poor girl was frantic. The palace was in an uproar. Servants ran for ladders. Hundreds of people at court saw the monkey sitting on top of the building. He was holding me like a baby in one of his forepaws, while feeding me with the other. He was cramming food into my mouth from a bag on one side of his little pants. Whenever I would not eat, he would pat me. At the sight of this, the crowd below could not help but laugh. I could understand why. Without question, it looked ridiculous to everybody but me. Some people threw stones, hoping to drive the monkey down. But others stopped them, afraid they might dash out my brains.

Ladders were raised and climbed by several men. The monkey saw them and realized he was almost surrounded. Needing the use of all four legs, he dropped me on the peak of the roof and made his escape. There I sat awhile, five hundred yards from the ground, expecting to be blown down by the wind or to fall due to my own dizziness. Finally, a brave lad climbed up, put me in a pocket, and brought me down safely.

I was nearly choking due to the filthy stuff the monkey had crammed down my throat. My dear little nurse picked it out of my mouth with a small needle. Then I vomited, which gave me great relief. I was so weak and bruised from the monkey's squeezes that I was forced to stay in bed for two weeks. The king, queen, and all the court inquired about my health every day. Her majesty paid several visits. The monkey was killed and a decree issued that no such animal should be kept in the palace.

I visited the king after my recovery to thank him for his many favors. He spent some time discussing my recent adventure. He asked me what I had been thinking as I lay in the monkey's paw, how I liked the food he gave me, if the fresh air on the roof had whetted my appetite. He wanted to know what I would have done if the same had happened to me in my own country. I told his majesty that in Europe the only monkeys we had were small, brought from distant countries as curiosities. I could easily defend myself against a dozen of them. I had been so frightened of the huge monkey that I forgot to draw my sword. Perhaps if I had wounded his paw, he would have pulled it out more quickly than he had put it in.

My speech made everyone sitting with the king laugh even though they should have contained themselves out of respect for his majesty. I realized I sounded like a person who was afraid his courage might be called in question. I realized it is useless to expect to be treated with respect by anyone far above your station in life. Sadly, since my return to England, I have been known to behave just as badly. It's so easy to disrespect someone without a title, or wit, or common sense, who presumes to consider himself equal to the greatest persons of the kingdom.

Every day I had some ridiculous story to relate at court. And Glumdalclitch, though she loved me to excess, would not hesitate to tell the queen about the latest foolish thing I'd done. Once, when the girl was sick, her governess took her to get some fresh air about an hour from town. They stepped out of the coach near a small footpath in a field and Glumdalclitch set down my traveling box. I went for a walk. There was cow-dung in the path and I simply had to try to leap over it. Though I took a running start, my jump fell short. I found myself up to my knees. I waded through with some difficulty. One of the footmen wiped me as clean as he could with his handkerchief. My nurse kept me in my box until we returned home. The queen soon learned what had happened because the footmen spread the story around. For a few days, all the jokes told at court were at my expense.

PART II
Chapter 6

I often watched the royal barber work on the king. It was, at first, very terrible to behold. The razor was almost twice as long as a scythe blade. His majesty, according to the custom, was shaved twice a week. I once convinced the barber to give me some of the used lather, out of which I picked forty or fifty of the strongest stumps of hair. I then took a piece of fine wood and cut it like the back of a comb. In it, I made a regularly spaced set of holes with the tiniest needle available. Using the king's hair, I made a reasonably useful comb. I was glad to have it, as many of the teeth in my comb had broken. No craftsman in that country could have made me one as fine.

Another time, I asked the queen's personal servant to save the combings from her majesty's hair. When I had collected enough, I consulted with my friend, the cabinet-maker. He completed a few jobs to my specification. He made two chair-frames to match those I had in my box. He used a very sharp awl to bore tiny holes in the backs and seats. Through these holes I wove the strongest hairs I could find, as they do with cane chairs in England. When they were finished, I presented them to her majesty. She kept them in her apartment and would sometimes show them off as curiosities. The queen wanted me to sit in one of these chairs, but I absolutely refused. I said I would rather die than place a dishonorable part of my body on hairs that once adorned her majesty's head. From these same hairs (I always had a talent for craft) I made a little purse, about five feet long, with her majesty's monogram in gold letters. I gave it to Glumdalclitch, with the queen's consent. To tell the truth, it was more for show than use, being too weak to bear the weight of their larger coins. Therefore she kept nothing in it but some little toys that girls enjoy.

The king, who loved music, frequently held concerts at court. Sometimes I was carried there and set in my box on a table to listen. Unfortunately, the noise was so loud I could hardly make out the melodies. All the drums and trumpets of a royal army, beating and sounding together right in your ears, could not equal the noise. I would have my box placed as far as possible from where the performers sat. If I then shut the doors and windows and drew the curtains, the music was not unpleasant.

I had learned in my youth to play the piano a little. Glumdalclitch kept one in her chamber, where she had lessons twice a week. I call it a piano, because it somewhat resembled that instrument and was played in the same way. I came up with the idea of entertaining the king and queen with an English tune. However, the piano was nearly sixty feet long and each key a foot wide. With my arms fully extended I could barely reach five keys. To press them down required a heavy blow with my fist, which would hardly be worth the effort. The method I devised was this: I prepared two large round sticks, thicker at one end than the other. I covered the thicker ends with pieces of mouse skin. Rapping them on the keys did no damage. A long bench was placed about four feet below the keyboard. I ran up and down as fast as I could, banging with my two sticks. I could only strike sixteen keys. The bass and treble could never be sounded together, a great disadvantage to my performance. I played a jig as best I could, to the great satisfaction of both their majesties. It turned out to be the most vigorous exercise I had ever attempted.

The king, an intelligent ruler, would frequently order that I should be brought in my box and set upon the table in his apartment. He would then command me to bring out one of my chairs and sit almost level with his face. In this manner, we had several conversations.

One day I felt confident enough to tell his majesty that the contempt he had towards Europe was out of character, considering his intellect. The king listened carefully. He asked me to provide an accurate account of the government of England. He hoped to gain some useful knowledge.

At that moment, I wished for the wisdom and words to describe my native country in the fashion it deserves. I began by informing his majesty, "Our empire consists of two islands within which are three mighty kingdoms, all ruled by one king. In addition, we have some colonies in America." I described at length the fertility of our soil and the mildness of our climate. I described our Parliament. "Some of its members make up that illustrious body called the House of Lords. They are of noble blood and inherit their posts." I described the extraordinary care taken in their education to prepare them to counsel the king and kingdom, share in creating laws, serve as judges, and defend king and country. Members of the House of Lords are the finest men of the kingdom who are never corrupt.

I went on to describe the clergy, called bishops, who join the House of Lords to take care of religious matters and instruct its members. The king and his counselors carefully select them as the wisest and holiest members of the clergy.

I discussed the other half of the Parliament, the House of Commons. The people freely select its members for their great abilities and love of country. Together, these two houses make up the most dignified assembly in Europe. They are completely responsible for our country's laws.

I moved on to the courts. I told the king how our judges wisely interpret the law and settle disputes about rights and property. In addition, they decide matters of guilt and innocence for our protection. I mentioned the ministers who carefully manage the country's money. I listed the achievements of our armed forces, by sea and land. I calculated the various segments of our population, how many members there were in each religious group and political party. I even covered our sports and hobbies, as well as any other detail that would reflect honorably on my country. I finished with a brief historical account of England for the past hundred years.

It took five interviews of several hours each to complete this conversation with the king. The king listened with great attention, frequently taking notes and jotting down questions he intended to ask.

During our sixth meeting, the king posed questions, doubts, and objections to almost everything I had said. He asked, "How are your young nobles educated? What happens if a particular noble family has no heirs? What qualifications were considered when choosing a new Lord? Was such a choice ever based on the whim of the king, money paid to marry a court lady, or a plan to strengthen the numbers of those opposed to the public interest? How much did these Lords actually know about the law? How did they acquire enough knowledge to enable them to make important and sometimes final decisions about their fellow citizens? Was the system designed so that these Lords were beyond influence from prejudice or bribes? Were those holy Lords of whom you spoke always chosen on the basis of their knowledge in religious matters and the purity of their lives? Or were they selected because they would do whatever those who chose them wanted?"

He then wanted to know, "How were the elections conducted for members of the House of Commons? Could someone influence the vote with money? Why would anyone want to become a member of this assembly when you described the post as a great trouble and expense with no salary or pension?" And he desired to know, "Would it be possible for a member of the House of Commons to sacrifice the public good in an effort to repay himself for all his troubles? Could he accomplish such misdeeds by working with corrupt ministers?" He asked questions about my answers and had many doubts that I think it better not to repeat.

In relation to what I said about our courts, his majesty had questions about several points. I felt more qualified to do so, since I had some experience. I had almost been financially ruined by a long suit in a high court, which was eventually decided in my favor, including court costs. He asked, "How much time is usually spent in deciding between right and wrong? At what cost? Are lawyers free to argue for a cause known to be unjust or cruel? Does membership in a particular political party or religion ever influence a decision? Are lawyers educated in ethics or only in local or national laws? Do lawyers or judges ever have any role in writing laws, which they might then feel free to interpret or ignore? Do lawyers ever argue—on different occasions—for and against the same cause, by citing previous cases to justify their contradictory opinions? Are judges rich or poor? Do lawyers or judges ever receive payment for pleading a case or delivering a judgment? Do judges or lawyers ever become members of the House of Commons?"

Next, he examined my discussion of the management of our treasury. He was sure my memory had failed me. I had figured our tax collections in England at about five or six million a year. Yet, as the king had continued to take notes on what I said, he was sure the costs I listed were twice that. If that were true, how could a kingdom spend more than it took in? He asked who our creditors are and where we found money to pay them. He wondered about the expensive wars I'd mentioned.

He thought we must certainly be a hot-tempered people or live in a very bad neighborhood. He added that our generals must be richer than our kings.

Most shocking of all, he had been amazed to hear that England employed professional soldiers. "Why keep a standing army in the midst of peace among a free people? If you are truly governed by your own consent," he asked, "of whom are you afraid? Would you rather have your house defended by people you know or by professionals who might be offered a hundred times more to cut your throats?"

He thought it very odd that I had divided our population into different religions and political parties. In his country no one has to reveal his religious beliefs or politics. If it is possible to count English people in that fashion, he reasoned, then it must be the law that everyone is required to make their private views public. What will then prevent powerful people from acting against people with whom they disagree?

He described my historical account of the last century in this way: nothing more than a heap of conspiracies, rebellions, murders, massacres, and revolutions. All of these were the effect of greed, hypocrisy, cruelty, rage, madness, hatred, envy, lust, and ambition.

His majesty attempted to sum up all I had said. He took me in his hand, stroked me gently, and said, "My little friend Grildrig, you have clearly proven that in your country ignorance, laziness, and vice, are the best qualifications for a legislator. You have shown that those who interpret your laws are those who have the most interest in perverting and avoiding them. Some of your country's institutions may once have had some good in them. Now they have become corrupted. Among your people virtue is no virtue. Priests are not advanced for their piety or learning. Soldiers are not advanced for their bravery, nor judges for their integrity, nor politicians for their wisdom or love of country. You," continued the king, "have spent the greatest part of your life traveling. I hope that means you have escaped the vices of your country. As for the rest of your natives, they appear to be the most spiteful race of revolting vermin ever to crawl on the face of the earth."

O_{nly} my extreme love of truth could have stopped me from keeping this part of my story secret. It was useless to voice my objections, which the king always ridiculed. I had no choice but to stay silent and listen to my country being insulted. I am as sorry as any of my readers can possibly be that I gave the king such a chance. But he asked so many questions about every detail that it would have been rude not to answer. In my own defense, I was able to dodge many of his questions. Almost every answer I did give, I put in a better light by shading the truth. I have always agreed with those historians who hide the shortcomings of the mother country and emphasize her virtues. This I tried to do in my discussions with the king. Unfortunately, I failed.

We should show some understanding to a king who lives completely isolated from the rest of the world. He is completely unfamiliar with the ways of other nations. Lacking such knowledge leads to a certain narrowness of thinking. Fortunately, we of England and Europe are completely immune from these prejudices.

My readers may find the following story hard to believe. I include it as a further example of what I have been saying about the king's isolation. To improve the king's opinion of me, I told him about a certain powder, discovered between three and four hundred years ago. I explained to him, "Should a tiny spark fall into a heap of this powder, the whole pile will ignite, even if it is as big as a mountain. This ignition can create an explosion louder than thunder. If the correct amount of this powder is rammed into a sufficiently large hollow metal tube, a ball of iron or lead can be projected from it with great force. The largest balls discharged in this way can destroy whole ranks of an army at once, batter down the strongest walls, and sink large ships. We often put this powder into large hollow balls of iron and discharge them into a city we are attacking. These balls rip up pavements, tear houses to pieces, and dash out the brains of everyone nearby. I know the ingredients for this powder. They are cheap and easily found. I can direct your majesty's workmen in constructing tubes the correct size for your majesty's kingdom. Twenty or thirty of these tubes, charged with the proper amount of powder and balls, could batter down the walls of the strongest town in the kingdom. They could destroy any city that disobeyed the your majesty's commands." This I humbly offered to the king in return for all I had received thanks to his royal favor and protection.

The king was horrified. How could "a power-less and groveling insect like you" (these were his exact words) "have such inhuman thoughts and be so insensitive to the death and destruction caused by those terrible machines? An enemy of humankind must have invented them in the first place. As for myself, though I usually delight in new discoveries, I would rather lose half my king-dom than share such a secret. I hereby command you, on pain of your life, never to mention it again."

What a strange result of his narrow thinking and the seclusion of his island! Here was a king with all the virtues we admire, possessed of great wisdom, adored by his subjects. And he was will-ing to refuse the opportunity give his people a tool that would guarantee their lives, their freedom, and their fortunes! I do not, in saying this, intend to disparage the many virtues of that excellent king, though I realize his reputation is now tar-nished among my English readers.

In Europe, politics is regarded as a science. When I told the king that, in our country, there are several thousand books about the art of govern-ment, he formed a poor opinion of our knowledge.

He claimed to despise court intrigue. He actually believed that governing meant using good sense and clear reasoning, dispensing justice, settling disputes in a timely manner, and other such notions not even worth considering. He declared that "the man who discovers how to make two ears of corn where only one grew before deserves a better reward and performs a more essential service to his country than all the politicians put together."

Education in Brobdingnag is substandard. Students learn only morality, history, poetry, and mathematics, and excel in each. They only study mathematics with useful applications, such as in agriculture and all engineering. Such knowledge is not held in high regard in our country. We value ideas, abstractions, and numbers that cannot be expressed with numerals.

No law in that country is permitted to use more than twenty-two words, the number of letters in their alphabet. But most are shorter. They are expressed in language so plain and clear, the law can be interpreted in only one way. In fact, writing a commentary on any law is a serious crime.

The people of Brobdingnag have used printing presses for centuries, yet their libraries are small. The king's collection, said to be the largest in the land, has less than a thousand volumes. It is housed in a gallery twelve hundred feet long. I had permission to borrow any books I wanted. The queen's carpenter designed a kind of wooden machine for my use in the library. Built like a standing ladder twenty-five feet high, it could be moved. The book I wanted would be leaned against the wall. I would climb to the top step. I would turn towards the book, beginning at the top of the page. I would walk right and left as I read, until I got below eye level. Then I would gradually descend until I came to the bottom. I would climb again and begin the next page in the same way. I could actually turn the pages myself, as they were thick and stiff and never more than twenty feet long.

As to their military, the king's army consists of a hundred and seventy-six thousand foot soldiers and thirty-two thousand cavalrymen. I hesitate to call it an army, however. It is made up of skilled workers and farmers. The commanders come from the upper class. Everyone serves without pay or reward.

I have often seen the militia of Lorbrulgrud exercising near the city in a great field about twenty miles square. There were less than twenty-five thousand foot soldiers and six thousand horsemen, but it was impossible for me to count them in such a large area. A cavalryman, mounted on a large steed, might be about ninety feet high. I have seen all of the mounted soldiers draw their swords at once and brandish them in the air. Imagination can

picture nothing as grand, as surprising, as astonishing! It looked like ten thousand flashes of lightning
darting at once from every quarter of the sky.

PART II
Chapter 8

I always had a strong feeling I would eventually recover my liberty, though it was impossible to imagine how. My ship was the first to sail within sight of that coast. The king had given strict orders that if another ship appeared it should be taken ashore. The crew and passengers would then be brought in a cart to Lorbrulgrud.

The king was determined to find a woman of my own size with whom I might breed. As for me, I would rather die than leave offspring to be kept in cages, like tame canary-birds, and perhaps, in time, sold to the wealthy as curiosities. Indeed, I had been treated with much kindness; I was the favorite of a great king and queen and the delight of the whole court. That attention, however, did not tend to enhance my dignity. In addition, I could never forget those I had left behind. I wanted to be among people with whom I could converse on equal terms. I wanted to walk about the streets and fields without the fear of being trod to death like a frog or a young puppy. But my deliverance came sooner than I expected and in a strange manner. I will tell the whole story in detail.

At the beginning of my third year in this country, Glumdalclitch and I went with the king and queen to the south coast of the kingdom. I was carried, as usual, in my traveling box. Inside, a hammock hung by silken ropes to soften the jolts when I was carried on horseback, as I sometimes requested. I would often sleep in my hammock while we were on the road. In the roof of my closet, but not directly over the middle of the hammock, I ordered the carpenter to cut a hole one foot square, to give me air in hot weather. I could shut the hole at any time with a board that slid backward and forward through a groove.

When we came to our journey's end, the king decided to spend a few days at a palace near Flanflasnic, a city eighteen miles from the seaside. Glumdalclitch and I were quite tired. I had gotten a small cold, but the poor girl was so ill she had to be confined to her room. I longed to see the ocean, my only means of escape. Pretending to be sicker than I was, I asked to take in the fresh air of the sea. A reliable young servant, of whom I was very fond, brought me there. I shall never forget with what unwillingness Glumdalclitch finally

agreed to let me go. I will always remember her telling the boy to be careful as she burst into tears. I now believe she had an intuition about what was to happen.

Carrying me in my box, the boy took me about half an hour from the palace, towards the rocks on the seashore. I ordered him to set me down. Lifting up one of my curtains, I cast many sad glances towards the sea. Feeling ill, I decided to take a nap in my hammock, which I hoped would do me some good. I got in, and the boy shut the window to keep out the cold.

I soon fell asleep, and all I can guess is that the young fellow, thinking no danger could happen, went searching for birds' eggs. In fact, I had noticed him earlier in the day looking around and picking up one or two eggs. Be that as it may, I found myself suddenly awakened by a violent pull on the ring fastened to the top of my box. I felt my box raised high in the air and carried with great speed. The first jolt nearly shook me out of my hammock, but afterwards the motion became smooth. I called out several times, as loud as I could, but all to no purpose. I looked towards my windows, and could see nothing but clouds and sky. I heard a noise just over my head, like the flapping of wings. Then, I began to understand the woeful condition I was in. Some eagle had gotten hold of the ring of my box in his beak. He intended to let it fall on a rock, like a tortoise in a shell, and then pick out my body and devour it.

In a little while, I noticed an increase in the noise and flutter of wings. My box began to be tossed up and down like a sign on a windy day. The eagle was itself battered about a few times. All of a sudden, I felt myself falling with such incredible swiftness that I almost lost my breath. The fall was stopped by a terrible squash louder to my ears than Niagara Falls. I was completely in the dark for a minute until my box began to rise and I could see light from the tops of the windows.

I had fallen into the sea. My box floated about five feet deep in water. I suppose the eagle had been pursued by two or three other eagles out to steal the prize he held in his beak. He must have been forced to let me drop while he defended himself against the rest. The plates of iron fastened at the bottom of the box preserved its balance while it fell and kept it from being broken when it hit the water. My box had been so well designed and constructed that very little water came in. I opened the hole in the roof to let in fresh air.

During my time in the sea, I often wished I were with my dear Glumdalclitch, from whom I had been separated by one simple decision! To tell the truth, even in the midst of my own misfortunes I could not help but weep for her. Not only would she be upset at losing me, but she was also likely to suffer from the queen's anger.

I was expecting my box to be smashed to pieces at any moment. If one single pane of glass had broken, it would have meant immediate death. I saw water oozing through several cracks. Thankfully, the leaks were not considerable. I stopped them as well as I could. Had I been able to get up on the roof and sit there, I certainly would have. I would probably have been able to survive there a few hours longer than if I remained shut in my box. Even if I escaped these dangers for a day or two, what could I expect but a miserable death of cold and hunger? After four hours of being trapped, I was expecting, and indeed wishing, every moment to be my last.

In the midst of entertaining these unhappy thoughts, I heard, or at least thought I heard, a noise coming from the windowless side of my box. There, as you may remember, two strong staples had been fastened for attaching the belt of any servant who carried me on horseback. Soon, I began to think that the box was being pulled or towed. I felt a sort of tugging now and then, which made the waves rise to the tops of my windows, leaving me almost in the dark. I began to have some faint hope of rescue although I could not imagine how that might happen. I climbed up on one of my chairs. Putting my mouth as near as I could to the opening in my roof, I called for help in a loud voice in every language I understood. Then I fastened my handkerchief to a stick and thrust it through the hole. I waved it several times in the air, hoping someone in a passing ship would realize that there was an unhappy man shut up in the box.

My efforts proved fruitless. However, it was clear that my box was being moved. In about an hour, the windowless side of the box struck something hard. I assumed it was a rock. I heard a grating noise like a cable passing through the ring on the roof. I found myself hoisted up slowly at least three feet higher than before. Once again, I held up my stick and handkerchief, calling for help till I was almost hoarse. In return, I heard a great shout repeated three times. Only someone who has felt as I did can understand my joy at that moment. I heard footsteps overhead. Then somebody called through the hole with a loud voice, and in English! "If there be anybody below, let them speak."

I answered, "I am an Englishman. The most unfortunate luck led me to this calamity. I beg you please deliver me from this dungeon."

The voice replied that I was safe. My box was fastened to the ship. "The carpenter will come soon and saw a hole. Then we will pull you out."

"That is not necessary. Just have one of the crew put his finger into the ring, lift up the box, and carry it into the captain's cabin." Some of them, hearing me talk so wildly, thought I was mad. Some laughed. I did not realize that I was now among people my own size. The carpenter came. In a few minutes he sawed a passage about four feet square. He let down a small ladder and I climbed out. I was taken aboard the ship in a very weak condition.

The sailors were amazed and asked me a thousand questions. I had no desire to answer at the moment. I was quite bewildered. The sight of so many tiny men confused me. I had become accustomed to living among giants. The captain, Mr. Thomas Wilcocks, a worthy gentleman, realized I was about to collapse. He took me into his cabin. He offered a medicinal glass of liquor and told me to take a little rest, of which I had great need. Before I went to sleep, I let him know I had some valuable furniture in my box, too good to be lost. There was a fine hammock, a handsome bed, two chairs, a table, and a cabinet. If he would simply let one of the crew bring my box into his cabin, I would show him everything. The captain concluded I was raving mad. However, to calm me down, he promised to order the crew to retrieve my belongings.

He went up on deck and sent some of his men down into my apartment. They gathered up all my goods. The chairs, cabinet, and bed frame were screwed to the floor. They were damaged by the ignorance of the seamen, who tore them up by force. The crew salvaged some of the wood from my box. Then, they let the rest drop into the sea. It now had many holes in it and sank immediately. I am glad not to have witnessed what happened. It would have upset me greatly. I would rather forget some of the memories that seeing it would have brought to mind.

I slept uneasily, disturbed by dreams of the place I had just left and the dangers I had escaped. However, when I awoke, I found myself much recovered. It was now about eight o'clock at night. The captain ordered supper immediately, thinking I had already fasted too long. He treated me with great kindness, noting that I no longer looked troubled or talked wildly. When we were left alone, he asked if I would tell him about my travels and explain how I came to be set adrift in that monstrous wooden chest. He said that about noon, as he was looking through his glass, he spied it in the distance. Thinking it was a ship, he decided to meet up with it, hoping to buy some needed supplies. When he got nearer, he sent out a boat. His men returned in a fright, swearing they had seen a swimming house. He laughed and went out himself, ordering his men to take a strong cable along. He rowed around me several times, noticing my windows and the wire that protected them. Then he noticed the two staples. He commanded his men to row up to that side. Fastening a cable to one of the staples, he ordered them to tow my chest—as they called it—to the ship.

There he gave directions to fasten another cable to the ring at the top. The sailors were ordered to raise the chest with pulleys. All of them together could only lift it two or three feet. He said they saw my stick and handkerchief and concluded that some unhappy man must be shut up inside.

I asked if he or the crew had seen any huge birds about the time that I was first spotted. In fact, while I was asleep he had talked to some sailors, one of whom mentioned noticing three eagles flying north. He said nothing about their being larger than the usual size. I thought to myself, "If they were flying high enough, they would not have looked remarkable to someone on shipboard." He could not, of course, guess the reason for my question. I asked the captain how far from land we were. His best computation indicated at least three hundred miles. I assured him he must be mistaken by almost half. I had only left the country from which I came about two hours before I dropped into the sea.

He began again to think that my brain was

disturbed and advised me to go back to bed. I tried to reassure him. But he grew serious and sought permission to ask some frank questions. He wanted to know if I had committed some terrible crime. Had I been punished by being abandoned in that chest? "In all honesty," the captain admitted, "I would be sorry such a criminal had come on board. But, I give my word I will put you ashore safely at the very first port." Some very bizarre statements I had made to the sailors aroused his suspicions when I first arrived. My strange chest and odd behavior at supper increased his mistrust.

"The only way to understand what happened to me is to hear the whole story," I said. I begged him to listen patiently. I told everything from the last time I left England to the moment that he first discovered me. Truth has great power. This honest gentleman, a man of good sense, was immediately convinced. But to confirm all I had said, I asked him to order my cabinet be brought. I had the key in my pocket.

I opened it in his presence and showed him the curiosities I had made in the country from which I had been so strangely delivered. There was the comb with stumps of the king's beard for teeth, four wasp stingers as big as ten penny nails, some combings of the queen's hair, and a gold ring, which she removed from her little finger, and threw over my head like a collar. I wanted the captain to accept this ring in return for his courtesy, but he absolutely refused. I showed him a corn about the size of a pippin apple that I had cut off with my own hand from a maid of honor's toe. It was so hard that I had it made into a cup and set in silver when I returned to England.

The captain refused every gift I offered except a servant's tooth, which I could tell he fancied. He thanked me more heartily than such a trifle deserved. An unskilled surgeon removed it by mistake from one of Glumdalclitch's men, who had a toothache. But it was as sound as any in his head. I got it cleaned and put it into my cabinet. It was about a foot long and four inches in diameter.

The captain was very well satisfied with my story and said he hoped, when we returned to England, I would make it public. I replied that we were overstocked with travel books. Besides, nothing is extraordinary anymore. So many authors do not bother with the truth. They write whatever they imagine or whatever will entertain ignorant readers. My story, I insisted, would not have any flowery descriptions of strange plants, trees, birds, or other animals. It would not show the primitive customs and idol worship of savages, which are the main topics these days. I thanked him, however, for his kind words and promised to think seriously about his suggestion.

He wanted very much to know why I spoke so loudly. He asked if the king or queen of that country were hard of hearing. I explained that, for more than two years, I constantly had to project my voice as if talking to someone at the top of a church steeple.

I told him I had realized something else. When I first got into the ship, and the sailors stood all about me, I thought they were the nastiest little creatures I had ever seen. In fact, while I was in that king's country, I could never bear to look in a mirror. Seeing so many huge objects made me feel unimportant. The captain had noticed that while we were eating supper, I looked at everything with a sort of disbelief. It seemed I could hardly contain my laughter. He considered this odd behavior one more sign of some disorder in my brain.

"It is very true," I said. "It was hard not to laugh when I saw dishes the size of silver coins, legs of pork hardly large enough for a mouthful, and a cup smaller than a nutshell." It is true the queen had provided everything I needed in a size I could use. But I was more fascinated by everything I saw around me. I forgot how small I was in the same way people forget about their faults.

The captain understood why everything here looked so odd to me. Quoting the old proverb, he said he doubted my eyes were bigger than my belly, for I had almost no appetite though I had fasted all day. He said, "I would have paid handsomely to see your box in the eagle's bill. Then, when it fell from such a great height, it must have been a most astonishing sight!"

Our voyage went quite smoothly, so I shall not trouble the reader with the details. The captain docked at one or two ports to send some crew members to buy food and fresh water. I never left the ship until we landed in England, about nine months after my escape. I offered to leave some things as security for payment of my freight, but the captain insisted I owed him nothing. We said goodbye after I made him promise he would come to see me in Redriff. I hired a horse and guide with money I borrowed from the captain.

On the road, the houses, trees, cattle, and people looked so small. I began to think I was in Lilliput again. Afraid of trampling every traveler I passed, I would scream at them to get out of the way. It's lucky no one gave me a good smack for my disrespect.

Finally, I arrived at my own house, after asking directions from a stranger. When one of the servants opened the door, I bent down to go in, afraid of striking my head. My wife ran out to embrace me, but I stooped lower than her knees, thinking she would never be able to reach my mouth. My daughter kneeled to ask my blessing, but I could not see her until she got up. I was too used to standing with my head and eyes looking up to a point sixty feet high. I looked down on the servants and my friends as if they were pygmies and I a giant. I told my wife she must have done too much penny-pinching. It looked as if she had starved herself and our daughter to nothing. In short, I behaved so strangely, that they all came to the same opinion as the captain. They were sure I had lost my wits. In time, however, I readjusted.

My wife swore I would never go to sea again. Destiny had other plans for me, however. Even my wife could not alter fate, as the reader will learn shortly. In the meantime, I here conclude the second part of my unfortunate voyages.

GULLIVER'S TRAVELS

PART III

A Voyage to the Country of The Houyhnhnms

PART III
Chapter 1

I stayed at home with my wife and children for about five months, quite happy. However, I had not changed. I was incapable of realizing when I was well off. I left my poor wife big with child and accepted a promising offer to captain a fine merchant ship.

After several of my men died of the fever, I was forced to find recruits wherever I could. I hired replacements on the island of Barbados, but soon came to regret that decision. Most of them were pirates.

My orders were to trade with the natives in the South Seas and make any discoveries I could. That mission was never accomplished. The scoundrels I had hired corrupted my crew. They rushed into my cabin and tied me hand and foot. They threatened to throw me overboard if I even stirred. I submitted. They fastened one of my legs to the

bed with a chain and placed a guard at the door.
His pistol was loaded. Their plan was to pirate
Spanish ships as soon as they could get some more
men. First, they would sell the goods aboard the
ship. Then they would go to Madagascar in search
of new crew members.

They sailed many weeks, but I do not know
what course they took, since I was a prisoner. On
the 9th day of May, 1711, one James Welch came
down to my cabin, and said, "I have orders from
the captain to put you ashore." I objected, but in
vain. He would not even tell me who this new captain was. They forced me into the longboat with
my best suit of clothes and a small bundle of linen,
but no weapons except my sword. Fortunately,
they did not search my pockets. There I had hidden all my money, along with some other trinkets
and necessities. They rowed about three miles then
set me down on a spit of land along the shoreline.
I asked what country it was. They all swore they
did not know. They did add, however, that the
captain had decided, once they sold the cargo, to
get rid of me the next time they spied land. They
pushed off immediately, warning me to move soon
since the tide was coming in.

In a dismal frame of mind, I got up and quickly reached solid ground. There, I sat down on a
bank to rest and consider my options. Refreshed, I
went inland, planning to surrender to the first savages I met. I had some bracelets, glass rings, and

other toys which might convince them to spare my life. As I walked, I noticed irregular rows of trees separating fields of grass and oats. I proceeded very carefully, fearing a surprise attack.

I chanced to find a well-used road with some footprints, some cow tracks, and many tracks of horses. At last, I saw several animals in a field, and one or two sitting among the trees. Their shape was very odd and rather deformed, which unnerved me. I lay down behind some under-growth to watch them. Some of them came near where I lay. Now I could see them more distinct-ly. Their heads and chests were covered with thick hair. They had beards like goats and a long ridge of hair down their backs and on the fronts of their legs and feet. The rest of their bodies were bare. Their skin looked browned by the sun. They had no tails and no hair on their buttocks, except at the very bottom. I suppose nature had placed it there to protect them as they sat on the ground. Indeed, I did see some sitting. Others were lying down. Still others were standing on their back feet. When they moved, these creatures proved to be very agile. They displayed a remarkable leaping ability. They climbed high trees as nimbly as squirrels using strong extended claws in front and behind. At the end of each claw were sharp, hooked points.

The females were not as large as the males. They had long, limp hair on their heads, but none on their faces. The rest of their bodies were covered

by nothing more than a sort of down-like fine hair. Among members of both sexes, I observed a variety of hair colors: brown, red, black, and yellow. On the whole, I had never before beheld such a disagreeable animal anywhere. Never before had I felt such natural disgust.

Thinking I had seen enough, I continued up the road, hoping to meet some natives. Instead, I met face to face with one of those awful creatures. The ugly monster made a variety of terrible faces and stared as if he had never before seen a creature like me. Coming closer, he lifted up his forepaw. I was not sure what he intended, so I drew my sword and hit him with the flat side. I dared not strike with the edge, fearing I might anger the inhabitants if they learned that I had killed or maimed one of their beasts. Feeling the pain from the blow, the creature drew back and roared so loudly that a herd of at least forty flocked around me. They were howling and making repulsive faces. I ran to a tree for protection. With my back against it, I kept them away by waving my sword. Several beasts leaped up into the tree. From there, they expelled their waste on my head. Very little fell on me, but I almost fainted from the filth that fell around my feet.

Suddenly, they all ran away. I immediately left the shelter of the tree and headed back to the road. I wondered what frightened them. Looking around, all I saw was a horse walking through a nearby field. I assumed, without understanding why, that the horse was the cause of their flight. The horse shied away when I first approached. Soon, however, he recovered and began looking at me very carefully. He examined my hands and feet, walking around me several times. I would have continued walking, but he placed himself directly in my way. I did not feel threatened, however. There was no suggestion of violence. We stood gazing at each other for some time. At last, I decided to make a friendly gesture. When experienced

English riders handle a strange horse, they whistle softly while gently stroking its neck. But this animal seemed to resent my attempt. He shook his head, wrinkled his brow, and softly raised up his right forefoot to remove my hand. Then he neighed three or four times with a neigh like none I had ever heard. I almost thought he was speaking in some language of his own.

Another horse came up. He greeted the first horse in a very formal manner. They gently struck each other's right hoof and neighed in a manner that made me think they were communicating. They went off together for a few minutes. They walked side by side, as if discussing something of importance. Often, they turned their eyes towards me, as if to make sure I would not escape. I was amazed to see such behavior in animals. I said to myself that, with horses this smart, the people here must be the wisest on earth. This thought gave me comfort. I decided I would keep going until I found a house or village or met up with some natives. As for the horses, they could chat as long as they liked. But when the first horse, a gray, noticed I was slipping off, he neighed after me so meaningfully I felt I understood him. I turned back and awaited further commands. I admit to having been somewhat fearful. I began to wonder what was going to happen. The reader will easily understand why I was ill at ease in that situation.

The two horses came near, looking at my face

and hands intensely. The gray steed felt my hat with his right fore-hoof so that I had to re-adjust it. Both he and his brown companion appeared to be much surprised. The brown felt the lapel of my coat and was amazed to find it hung loosely about me. He stroked my right hand, admiring the softness and color. But he squeezed it so hard that I roared. After that, they always touched me tenderly. They were completely perplexed by my shoes and stockings. They felt them often, neighing to each other and gesturing like scientists attempting to explain some baffling phenomenon.

On the whole, the behavior of these animals was so logical, so wise, I concluded they must be magicians. They had changed their shape, I speculated, when they saw me, a stranger. They had been amazed at the sight of a man so very different from those living here. On the basis of this line of thinking, I attempted to greet them.

"Gentlemen, if you are magicians—as I have reason to believe—you can probably understand my language. I am a poor unhappy Englishman, stranded in your country. I beg one of you to let me ride on his back, as if he were a real horse, to some house or village where I can find relief. In return, I will make you a present of this knife and bracelet." I took them out of my pocket. The two creatures stood silently while I spoke, listening. When I finished, they neighed frequently to each other, as if they were engaged in serious conversation.

I could frequently distinguish the word *yahoo*, which they repeated several times. As they chatted busily, I practiced this word. When they were silent, I boldly pronounced, "Yahoo," in a loud voice, imitating, as near as I could, the neighing of a horse. They were both visibly surprised. The gray repeated the same word again, as if to teach me the correct pronunciation. I echoed him as best I could. His friend tried teaching me a second word, much harder to pronounce. Using the English system, it would be spelled *Houyhnhnm*. I did not succeed in saying it as well as the first word, though I did improve after two or three attempts. They were both very impressed.

After further conversation, which I was convinced related to me, the two friends said goodbye as they had greeted each other, by striking hooves. The gray signaled that I should walk in front of him. I thought it sensible to comply, till I could find a better leader. Whenever I slowed down a bit, he would cry, "*Hhuun hhuun.*" I guessed his meaning, and tried to explain that I was weary and unable to walk faster. Then he stopped awhile to let me rest.

Three miles down the road, we came to a long structure built on a frame of timber stuck in the ground. The walls were made of interwoven branches. The roof was low and covered with straw. I felt reassured at last and took out some trinkets travelers use as presents for the natives of America and other lands. In this way, I hoped the people of the house would welcome me. The horse signaled for me to go in first. I entered a large room with a smooth clay floor. A trough extended the length of one side. Three older horses and two young females sat nearby, which I considered very odd. Even more peculiar, other horses around the room were doing various chores. This seemed to confirm my opinion that any nation that could civilize horses to this degree, must be the wisest in the world. The gray came in just then, ruling out the possibility that I would be mistreated by any of the other horses. He neighed several times in a voice of authority and received some replies.

Beyond this room were three others, extending to the end of the house. Three doors, opposite one another, created an open corridor between the rooms. We went through the second room to the third. The gray entered, motioning for me to follow. I stopped briefly in the second room, alone. There, I prepared presents for the hosts who surely awaited me: two knives, three bracelets of imitation pearls, a small mirror, and a bead necklace.

The horse neighed three or four times. Expecting a human voice to respond, I heard instead more neighing, a little shriller than the gray's. This house must belong to some person of importance, I thought, to require so much ceremony before I could enter. But, it was beyond belief to imagine a man of quality served completely by horses.

I looked around the room. Furnished like the first, it was a bit more elegant. I rubbed my eyes and pinched my arms, hoping I was dreaming. I concluded, once and for all, that everything I'd witnessed was the result of magic. But I had no time to pursue this line of thought. The gray horse came to the door and made a sign to follow him into the third room. There I saw a beautiful mare. Together with a colt and foal, she sat on her haunches on a well constructed mat of straw, perfectly neat and clean.

The mare rose and approached me carefully, observing my hands and face. She gave me a scornful look. Turning to the gray, she spoke the word *yahoo*, among others. I knew how to say the word, at that point, but did not understand what it meant. I would come to understand much better, in a moment.

The gray motioned with his head, repeating, "*Hhuun, hhuun.*" He led me into a kind of courtyard. There stood another building, some distance from the house. Entering, I saw three of those detestable creatures I had encountered after landing. They were feeding on roots and the flesh of some animals. I learned later the meat was from donkeys, dogs, and the occasional cow, killed by accident or disease. Each beast wore a halter around its neck. Each halter was tied to a beam. They held their food between the claws of their front feet and tore it with their teeth.

The master horse ordered one of his servants to untie the largest of these creatures. The beast and I were brought close together. Both master and servant compared our faces in detail, often repeating, "*Yahoo.*" Imagine my horror when I realized that this abominable animal was actually a human. The face, though broader, was not so different from mine. The front feet of the yahoo were exactly like my hands except for the long nails, the rough palms, and the hair on top. Our feet were likewise alike, something the horses did not realize because of my shoes and stockings.

The horses had no understanding of clothing and this contributed to their confusion. The servant horse offered me a root. I took it in my hand, smelled it, and placed it back in his hoof as politely as I could. He brought out of the yahoos' kennel a piece of donkey meat, but it smelled so bad I turned away in disgust. A yahoo greedily devoured it instead. Next, he showed me a tuft of hay and a few oats. I shook my head to indicate that neither of these were food for me. I began to worry that I might starve if I did not meet some of my own species.

There were few greater lovers of mankind at that time than me. But I considered the filthy yahoos completely detestable. In fact, my loathing for yahoos became greater the longer I stayed in that country. The master horse recognized my uneasiness and sent the yahoo back to his kennel. Imagine my surprise when the gray put his front hoof to his mouth. Clearly, he was attempting to discover what I would eat. I was unsure how to answer in a way he could understand. At that moment, I noticed a cow passing by. I pointed to her and made a motion as if I were milking her. This had the intended effect. He led me back to the house. A servant opened a storehouse of milk in vessels of clay and wood. She gave me a large bowl full. I drank very heartily and found myself refreshed.

About noon, I saw a vehicle approach the house. It was rather like a large sled pulled by four yahoos. In it was an old steed, treated with great respect by the other horses. He got off the sled hind feet first, due to an injury to his left front foot. He had come to dine with my horse, who greeted him courteously. They ate in the best room and had oats boiled in milk for the second course. They sat on their haunches at troughs placed in a circle. In the middle was a large rack with a section for each trough, so each horse ate his own hay and his own mash of oats and milk. The young colt and foal were well behaved. The master and mistress of the house were extremely cheerful and anxious to please their guest. The gray ordered me to stand near him. He and his friend discussed me at length. The stranger often looked at me and both frequently repeated the word *yahoo*.

I happened to be wearing my gloves. The two horses were at a loss to understand what I had done to my front feet. The gray touched the gloves with his hoof three or four times as if he wanted me to change my front feet back to their former shape. I did so. I pulled off both gloves and put them into my pocket. They continued talking and I could tell they were pleased with my behavior. I was ordered to say the few words I understood. As they ate, the master taught me the words for oats, milk, fire, water, and some others.

When dinner was done, the master horse took me aside. Using signs and words he let me know his concern that I had nothing to eat. Oats in their tongue are called *hlunnh*. This word I pronounced two or three times. I had refused oats at first but then realized I could survive on oat bread and milk until I was once again with creatures of my own species. The horse immediately ordered a servant to bring me a good quantity of oats in a sort of wooden tray. I heated the oats in the fire as best I could, rubbed them until the husks came off, and then separated the husks from the grain. I ground and beat them between two stones. Using water, I made them into a paste or cake, which I toasted on the fire and ate warm with milk.

In time, I got used to this bland diet. I must admit that I was never sick even once the whole time I stayed on this island. I was able to supplement my diet by catching rabbits and birds in traps made of yahoo hairs. I also gathered herbs, which I boiled and ate with my bread. Now and then, for a treat, I made a little butter.

This is more than enough to say on the subject of diet. I know other travel writers fill page after page describing everything they ate, as if readers actually care if we fare well or poorly. I felt it was necessary, in this case, to at least mention my diet. Otherwise, readers would certainly wonder how anyone could manage for three years in such a country, among such inhabitants.

Towards evening, the master horse provided a place for me to sleep only six yards from the house and completely separate from the stable of the yahoos. I was given straw to use as a bed. I covered myself with my own clothes and slept very soundly. In a short time I was given better accommodations. The reader will learn the details later, when I write at length about my style of life on the island.

My primary goal was to learn their language. It resembles German more than any other European tongue, though I think it is more graceful and expressive. My master (as I will call him from this point on), his children, and every servant wanted very much to teach me. They considered me a wonder, a brute animal with the characteristics of an intelligent being. I pointed to things and asked the names of them. I learned that the word *Houyhnhnm*—'horse' in English—comes from their word meaning "the perfection of nature." Everyone in the family helped improve my accent by frequently pronouncing any words I was learning. I translated everything I learned into the English alphabet. I jotted down the words and their meanings. The first time I wrote in my master's presence, I spent a great deal of time explaining what I was doing. The Houyhnhnms have no books, no concept of literature.

My master, anxious to hear my whole story, spent many hours instructing me. Convinced I was a yahoo, he was astonished by my good manners, cleanliness, and ability to learn. My clothes greatly perplexed him. I never pulled them off until the family was asleep. I put them back on before they awoke. My master kept wondering whether or not the clothing was part of my body.

In about ten weeks, I could understand most of his questions. In three months, I could give him adequate answers. My master was extremely curious to know where I came from and how I learned to imitate intelligent beings. Yahoos, he said, were the most unteachable of all brutes.

I told him I came by sea from a far place, with many others of my own kind, in a great hollow vessel made of the bodies of trees. I explained that my companions forced me to land on this coast and then left me. With some difficulty, and by using many signs, I helped him understand me. He replied, "You must be mistaken, or you have said the thing which was not." They have no word in their language for 'lie.' "There is no country beyond the sea. And beasts could never control a wooden vessel on water. No Houyhnhnm alive could make such a vessel. Certainly, no yahoo could be in charge of it."

I told my master I still lacked the words to

provide a full explanation. Not only did he order his entire family—and even the servants—to take every opportunity to instruct me, he began tutoring me on a regular basis, two or three hours a day.

Important local horses and mares often came to our house. They had heard the rumors about "a wonderful yahoo" that could speak like a Houyhnhnm, and seemed to be able to reason, in a limited way. These neighbors loved chatting with me. They posed many questions. I answered as best I could. Five months after my arrival, I understood whatever was said and could express myself fairly well.

None of our frequent visitors could believe I was a genuine yahoo, because my body had a different covering from others of my kind. They were astonished to observe me without the usual hair or skin, except on my head, face, and hands. Unfortunately, I eventually gave away the secret, quite by accident.

I have already told the reader that every night, after the family had gone to bed, I would strip and cover myself with my clothes. Early one morning, my master sent his personal servant to get me. He found me fast asleep. My blanket of clothes had fallen off to one side. My shirt was above my waist. He was so shocked, he made a noise that awoke me. He attempted to deliver the master's message but I could not understand him. He returned to my master in a great fright and gave a very confused account of what he had seen. This I discovered soon enough. As soon as I called on his honor, he ordered me to explain what his servant had reported. "He claims you are not the same thing asleep as you are at other times. He said part of you is white, some yellow, and some brown."

I had concealed the secret of my clothing to make a distinction between me and that cursed race of yahoos. I could do so no longer. Besides, I realized my clothes and shoes would soon wear out. Eventually they would have to be replaced with hides from yahoos or other animals. Then, everyone would know my secret. Therefore, I explained that in my country, humans always covered their bodies with the hairs of certain animals. These hides were decorative, allowed for decency, and protected us from the weather. If it pleased him, I was willing to provide immediate proof, with the understanding that I would not expose those parts nature taught us to conceal. He said, "All you have said is very strange, most especially the last part. Why would nature teach us to conceal what nature had given? Neither my family nor I are ashamed of any parts of our bodies. However, you can do as you please." I unbuttoned my coat and pulled it off. I removed my shoes, stockings, and pants. I turned my undershirt down to my waist and pulled up the bottom to hide my nakedness.

My master watched with signs of curiosity and admiration. He lifted up each piece of clothing and examined it carefully. He stroked my body very gently and walked around me several times. "You are a genuine yahoo! But you differ from your species. Your skin is soft, smooth, and white. You lack hair on several parts of your body. Your claws are shorter. You walk on two feet. I do not need to see any more. I can tell you are cold. You may put on your clothes again."

I told my master it made me uncomfortable to be called a yahoo. I had nothing but hatred and contempt for those revolting animals. I requested he no longer apply the term to me. I also asked that he order his family and friends to do the same. Lastly, I begged that he (and his personal servant) keep secret the false covering to my body for as long as my present clothing should last.

My master very graciously agreed to everything. In the meantime, he told me to continue working hard to learn their language, because he was more astonished than ever at my ability to speak and reason. He still looked forward impatiently to hearing the wonders I had promised to disclose.

From that moment on, he increased his efforts to instruct me. He insisted I join him whenever he had company. He was firm in asking his guests to regard me with courtesy. He told them such treatment would put me in a better mood and make me more entertaining.

Every day my master would ask several questions. I always answered as well as I could. In this way, he already had some general ideas about my background. Eventually, I was able to give the following extended account of my history.

"I came from a distant country," as I had already attempted to tell him, "with about fifty more of my own species. We traveled on the sea in a great hollow vessel made of wood, larger than his honor's house." I described the ship to him as best I could. By blowing into a handkerchief, I demonstrated the principle of wind power. I went on to explain how, after a quarrel among us, I was left behind on this coast.

He asked, "Who made the ship? How could the Houyhnhnms of your country leave the ship to the management of beasts?" I told him then I would not proceed with my story unless he gave me his word that he would not be offended. He agreed. I assured him that creatures exactly like me had made the ship. In fact, in every country I had ever visited, except his, humans were the only governing, intelligent animals. Furthermore, when I arrived in this country, I was as shocked to see Houyhnhnms acting like intelligent beings, as he, or his friends, would be, finding intelligence in the creatures they call yahoos. Though I did indeed resemble yahoos in many ways, I could not explain their brutal nature. I added that if good fortune ever restored me to my native country and I told about my travels here, no one would believe me. They would say I invented the story.

As my master listened he appeared to become uneasy. The inhabitants of his country are unaccustomed to doubting anyone's word. My master had great difficulty understanding the concept of lying. "The purpose of speech," he said, "is to make us understand one another and to receive information. If anyone says the thing which is not," the Houyhnhnms, remember, had no word for lie, "this purpose would be defeated. If he says the thing which is not, I cannot properly understand him. He has left me in a state worse than ignorance. I am led to believe a thing black when it is white, or short when it is long." This was his best understanding of lying, a skill so universally recognized and so skillfully practiced among human creatures.

When I declared that yahoos were the only governing animals in my country, my master asked, "Do you have Houyhnhnms among you? What do they do?"

I told him, "We have great numbers of Houyhnhnms. In summer, they graze in the fields. In winter they stay in houses well supplied with hay and oats. There, yahoo servants rub their skins smooth, comb their manes, serve them food, and keep their beds in order."

"I understand you well," said my master. "It is now quite clear. Though the yahoos in your country act as if they can reason, the Houyhnhnms are the masters. I wish we could train our yahoos as well."

I begged his honor, "Please excuse me from continuing. I am certain you will find the information I give highly displeasing."

But he insisted I tell everything. I continued. "Our Houyhnhnms, whom we call horses, are the most gentle and handsome of animals. They excel in strength and speed. When they belong to fine, wealthy yahoos they are used for traveling, racing, and pulling carriages. They are treated with kindness and well cared for until they become weak, sick, or too old. Then they are sold and used in any way they can until they die. Then their skin is removed and sold and their bodies are left to be devoured by dogs and birds of prey. The horses of the poor are not so fortunate. Farmers and laborers work them hard and feed them terribly."

I described riding and the equipment we use:

bridles, saddles, spurs, whips. I added, "We fasten plates of a certain hard substance, called iron, to the bottom of our horses' feet. In this way, we keep their hooves from being broken as we travel."

My master was highly offended. He could not understand how anyone could dare climb on a Houyhnhnm's back. For one thing, he was confident the weakest Houyhnhnm would shake off the strongest yahoo. I explained how our horses are trained. "Young horses that misbehave are severely beaten. Male horses are often castrated to make them more tame and gentle. Our horses do understand reward and punishment, but they cannot reason any more than yahoos in this country."

Houyhnhnms have no knowledge of the needs and passions we experience. Therefore, their language lacks many of the words I needed to give my master a complete picture of life in England. However, his honor had no problem expressing his resentment at our savage treatment of Houyhnhnms. He agreed that in any country where the yahoo was the only reasoning animal, it would certainly become the governing animal. Over time, reason always prevails over brute strength. But he considered the structure of our bodies, and especially mine, ill suited for using that reason to accomplish important tasks. He asked, "Do the yahoos of your country bear a closer resemblance to you or the yahoos of my country?"

I assured him, "I am as well shaped as most of

my age. The young and the females are much more soft and tender. The skin of our women is generally as white as milk."

He said, "You differ greatly from our yahoos. You are cleaner and not nearly as deformed. But, many other differences put you at a disadvantage. Your nails are of no use. You've lost the ability to walk on your front feet. In fact, I can hardly call them feet because you never walk on them. As a result, you walk hesitantly. If either of your back feet should slip, you fall."

Next, he began to find fault with other parts of my body. "Your face is flat. Your nose is prominent. Your eyes are placed so that you cannot look to the side without turning your head. You cannot feed yourself without lifting one of your front feet to your mouth. Your feet are too soft to endure rough ground without a covering made from the skin of some other animal. Every day you have to cover your whole body to protect it from heat and cold. Every animal in this country feels nothing but disgust toward yahoos. Weak creatures avoid them. Strong creatures drive them away. Even if yahoos had the power of reason, how would it be possible to cure that natural revulsion? How could yahoos ever gain control over animals that hated them? But let us stop debating this matter. I am much more interested in you and your country."

I assured him, "I very much want to give you a satisfactory account of my country and my history.

But I doubt it will be possible to discuss certain subjects. In your country you have no conception of them. Therefore, I have found nothing in this country to which they can be compared. Nevertheless, I will do my best, and ask for help when I lack the proper words.

"I was born of honest parents on an island called England. It is many days journey from your country. My country is governed by a female, whom we call queen. I learned to be a surgeon. A surgeon cures wounds and hurts gotten by accident or violence. I left my country to get money to support my family. On my last voyage, I was commander of the ship. About fifty yahoos served under me. Many of them died at sea and I was forced to hire sailors from other nations to take their places. Twice our ship was in danger of being sunk, the first time by a great storm and the second by striking against a rock."

Here my master stepped in. "How could you persuade strangers from foreign countries to go with you, considering the hazards and risks?"

I answered, "They were desperate men, forced to flee from their homes because of their poverty or their crimes. Some were ruined by lawsuits. Others spent all their money drinking and gambling. Some fled after committing crimes: treason, murder, theft, desertion. Many had escaped from prison. If any one of them returned to his native country, he would likely be hanged."

During this discussion, my master interrupted several times. I had been very indirect in describing several of the crimes committed by most of our crew. This task took up several days' conversation. He had been at a loss to appreciate the benefit of practicing such vices. I attempted to give him some idea of the desire for power and riches as well as the terrible effects of lust, drunkenness, and envy. For each, I gave examples. When my master understood, it was as if he were discovering something for the first time. He would raise his eyes in amazement and righteous anger. My master's language has no word for *power, government, war, law, punishment*. Yet, at last, he came to understand human nature in our part of the world.

Then he asked me to provide an account of that land we call Europe and especially of my own country.

PART III
Chapter 5

The conversations with my master occurred over a period of more than two years. As you might expect, the following are only extracts, summaries of the most important points.

On this occasion, I tried to convey a general impression of Europe. I discussed trade, manufacturing, science, and the arts. The master had many questions. Each answer spurred additional conversation. I could not include here every word of our conversations, but what I have included meets my aim of strictly adhering to the truth. My only fear is that I will not do justice to my master's arguments in summarizing them and translating them into our crude English.

I discussed the long war with France in which the greatest powers of Christendom were engaged, and which still continues. I estimated, at his request, that about a million yahoos might

have been killed, a hundred or more cities taken, and five times as many ships burnt or sunk.

He asked me to explain the usual motives for one country to go to war with another. I answered, "They are infinite. But I will list a few of the chief reasons. Princes never think they have enough land or people to govern. Corrupt ministers can bring about a war to divert attention from their evil. Differences in opinions have cost millions of lives. They may disagree whether flesh is bread, or bread is flesh, whether the juice of a certain berry is blood or wine, or the best color for a coat. In fact, the bloodiest and longest wars are fought over differences of opinion.

I went on to say to him, "Sometimes two princes quarrel over who owns some land to which neither has a right. Sometimes one prince quarrels with another for fear the other will quarrel with him. Sometimes a war is entered into because the enemy is too strong and, sometimes, because he is too weak. Sometimes our neighbors want the things we have or have the things we want. We fight till they take ours or give us theirs. It is just to invade a country after the people have been weakened by famine or civil war. We enter into war against our closest ally, if we can conveniently take some of his land. If you conquer a land where the people are poor and ignorant, you may lawfully put half of them to death and make slaves of the rest. In this way, we civilize them. It is very kingly to make a treaty with a prince whose land has been invaded. When the invader is removed, it is also very kingly to seize the lands of the prince whom you came to assist. Families often fight among themselves. In fact, the closer the relationship, the more likely they are to quarrel. For these reasons, the trade of soldier is considered the most honorable. A soldier is a yahoo hired to kill, in cold blood, as many of his own species, who have never offended him, as he possibly can.

"There are also some princes in Europe, too poor to make war by themselves, who hire out their troops to richer nations. They charge so much per day for each man. They keep three-fourths of the money for themselves. That money represents most of their income."

"Your discussion of war," said my master, "shows quite clearly what happens when yahoos can reason. Fortunately, nature has left your species unable to do much damage. With your flat mouths, you can't bite very well. Your front and rear claws are so short and tender that one of our yahoos could defeat a dozen of yours. Therefore, I believe you have said the thing which is not when you told me how many yahoos have been killed in battle."

I simply had to shake my head and smile at my master's ignorance. As I am quite familiar with the art of war, I proceeded to give him a complete description of: cannons, muskets, pistols, bullets, gunpowder, swords, bayonets, battles, sieges, retreats, attacks, mines, bombardments, sea fights, ships sunk with a thousand men, twenty thousand killed on each side, dying groans, limbs flying in the air, smoke, noise, confusion, flight, victory, fields strewn with corpses, plundering, burning, and destroying. To highlight the bravery of my own dear countrymen, I told of them blowing up a hundred enemies at once. The sight of the dead dropping down in pieces from the clouds provided great entertainment for the spectators. I had other tales to tell as well.

My master commanded me to be silent. He understood that no good could result from combining the natural strength and cruelty of yahoos with intelligence. But he was now experiencing an entirely new emotion. "Yes," he admitted, "I hate the yahoos of this country. But I never blame them for their disgusting behavior. Can I blame a sharp stone for cutting my hoof? Does the behavior of Europe's yahoos prove that corrupted intelligence is worse than natural brutality? No, these yahoos could not have true intelligence, just something resembling it. Instead, they have some quality that increases their natural faults.

"I have heard too much about war. There is another point that has been bothering me. You told me that some of your crew left their country after being ruined by the law. You have already explained the meaning of the word *law*. I am at a loss to understand how a law intended for every man's preservation, could be any man's ruin. Please tell more about what you mean by law. Describe those responsible for dispensing the law. Please provide details about how law is practiced in your country. Here, we simply use nature and reason as our guide in showing us what to do and what to avoid."

I had to tell his honor, "I have not had much to do with the law. All I really know about are the injustices that have been done to me." However, I promised to attempt a satisfactory explanation.

I said, "Some men among us are highly trained in the art of proving that white is black or black is white, depending on who is paying them.

For example, if my neighbor wants my cow, he hires a lawyer to prove that he deserves that cow. Then I hire a lawyer to defend me. (It is against all rules of law for a man to be allowed to speak for himself.) In this particular case I, as the lawful owner, have two great disadvantages. First, my lawyer, practiced in the art of defending falsehood, will find it quite unnatural to represent the truth. Second, my lawyer must proceed with great caution. If he behaves too honorably, he will be scolded by the judge and sneered at by his fellow lawyers. They will accuse him of undermining the practice of the law.

"In the end, I have only two methods for keeping my cow. I can pay my neighbor's lawyer double. He will then betray his client. Or, I can instruct my lawyer to make my cause appear as unjust as he can, admitting that the cow belongs to my enemy. If he can do so with enough skill, he will gain the support of the judge.

"Your Honor should know that judges are appointed to decide all arguments over property and crime. They are selected from among the most skillful lawyers, who have grown old or lazy. To qualify, they must show a strong bias against truth and justice. They stand firmly on the side of fraud, lies, and intimidation. In fact, some judges refuse large bribes from the side whose cause is just, rather than doing something ill suited to their nature or their office.

"Lawyers work hard to avoid discussing the case itself. Instead, they are loud, violent, and boring in speaking of everything else. Take, for instance, the case already mentioned. The lawyer will never ask what claim my opponent has to my cow. Instead, he asks if said cow were red or black, or her horns long or short. The judge will adjourn the case from time to time and in ten, twenty, or thirty years, come to a decision.

"In the trial of someone accused of crimes against the state, the method is much shorter. The judge merely finds out what those in power think. Then he can quickly hang or save the criminal, thereby preserving all the traditions of law."

Here my master broke in, saying, "Such gifted creatures as these lawyers should be encouraged to instruct others in wisdom and knowledge." I assured his Honor that in anything but the law, lawyers are known to be the most ignorant and stupid among us.

PART III
Chapter 6

My master was completely unable to understand what could motivate lawyers to behave so abominably merely to injure their fellow yahoos. He also had no concept of what I meant when I said they did it for hire. As a result, I spent time carefully explaining money to him. I told him that with a great deal of this precious money a yahoo could buy whatever he wanted: the finest clothing, the best houses, the most expensive food. Women would show greater interest in him. Only money could do this. Therefore our yahoos think they can never have enough. I explained how the rich live off the labor of the poor. I described the miserable lives of the majority of our people. Millions labored every day, for almost nothing, so a few yahoos could live grandly.

His Honor was unable to understand. He believed all animals deserved their share, especially the ruling species. Therefore, he wanted to know more about the expensive foods I had mentioned. He asked what they were and how anyone came to want them. So I listed as many as came into my head. I told how they were served. I explained that ships had to sail all over the world for liquors and spices. I assured him it takes three trips around the world to supply one wealthy female yahoo's breakfast.

He said, "That must be a miserable country which cannot furnish food for its own inhabitants." I replied that England produces three times more food than its inhabitants are able to eat. But, in order to feed the greed of its males and the vanity of its females, we send our necessities to other countries. In return, they send us what we need to increase disease, foolishness, and sin. As a result, vast numbers of our people make their living by begging, robbing, stealing, cheating, forging, gambling, lying, writing, astrology, prostitution, and other jobs of that sort. It took much discussion to help my master understand all those terms.

I explained that wine was not imported from foreign countries to quench our thirst. It makes us merry by putting us out of our senses, causing wild delusions in the brain, raising our hopes, driving away our fears, preventing us from thinking properly, and depriving us of the use of our arms and legs until we fall into a deep sleep. I confessed, however, that we always wake up sick and sad. In addition, the use of liquor causes diseases that make our lives uncomfortable and short.

I explained that most of our people support themselves by supplying each other with what they need or want. When I am dressed in my usual clothing, I carry on my body the products of a hundred workers. It takes that many, as well, to build and furnish my house. And it takes five times as many to beautify my wife.

I started to tell my master about people who earn their livelihood helping the sick. But he could not understand the concept of sickness. He knew that Houyhnhnms grew weak a few days before their death. He knew that sometimes an accident injured a Houyhnhnm. But he could not believe that nature would ever cause diseases to breed in otherwise healthy yahoos.

I told him, "It is our own fault. We eat when we are not hungry and drink when we are not thirsty. We spend whole nights drinking strong liquor without eating a bit. Certain female yahoos have a disease that rots the bones of those who fall into their embraces. A number of diseases are spread from father to son. As a result, many yahoos are born with complicated diseases.

"It would take too long to name every human disease. There must be at least five or six hundred, affecting every part of the body inside and out. To cure these maladies, we train people in the profession, or deception, of curing the sick. And because

I have some skill in the art, I will gladly let your honor know our secrets and methods.

"Our healers, also known as physicians, believe all diseases arise from excess. So they conclude that an emptying of the body is necessary. This emptying can take place through the usual passage or from the mouth. Using herbs, minerals, gums, oils, shells, salts, juices, seaweed, excrement, tree bark, serpents, toads, frogs, spiders, dead men's flesh, birds, beasts, and fishes, they create the most repulsive combinations possible. Of course, the stomach immediately rejects such potions. This they call a vomit. Some potions may be taken in through the mouth or the opening below, depending on the mood of the doctor. Taken below, the potion relaxes the belly and drives everything out. This they call an enema. These physicians know that nature intended the mouth for the entry of food and the opposite end for its exit. But they also believe that any disease reverses what is natural. Therefore, the body must be treated completely opposite from what is natural. These healers force solids and liquids into the bottom opening to make things come out of the mouth.

"Not only do physicians cure real diseases, they have also invented imaginary cures for imaginary diseases. They have drugs for each of these. Our female yahoos are also subject to these imaginary ills.

"The greatest skill possessed by doctors is

their ability to predict the outcome of serious diseases. Even when they lack the ability to cure a patient, they are quite capable of recognizing the terrible symptoms of a fatal disease. Should a patient unexpectedly show signs of recovery, they know how to prescribe the correct dose of something to prove their initial diagnosis correct. This skill is especially useful when the doctor is being paid by a husband or wife tired of a mate, a son waiting for his inheritance, a government minister, or a king."

I had already spoken to my master at length about government. But since I had, by chance, mentioned the term "government minister," he requested that I describe that kind of yahoo.

I told him, "Government ministers never experience joy and grief, love and hatred, or pity and anger. The only emotion they ever feel is a violent desire for wealth, power, and titles. They only tell the truth when they want you to think they are lying. They only lie when they want you to believe them. Anyone they criticize privately is in line for a promotion. Anyone they praise is sure to suffer. The worst thing that can happen is to have a government minister make you a promise, especially when he gives his solemn word. When that happens, anyone with any sense gives up hope and retires.

"There are three ways to become chief minister. The first is by knowing how to get rid of a wife, a daughter, or a sister without getting caught. The second is by betraying the minister for whom you work. The third is by publicly protesting corruption. Wise kings appoint such people because those who are the most passionate critics always make the most obedient ministers.

"Once appointed, the minister has the power to do many things. He keeps himself in office with bribes for as long as he can. When bribes fail to work, he awards himself a large pension and retires.

"At the palace of a chief minister, other ministers are trained. Errand boys, servants, and caretakers imitate their master. Eventually they become local ministers. In that position, they learn the minister's three essential skills: disrespect, lying, and bribery. With the proper combination of cleverness and rudeness, they sometimes replace their masters. Most chief ministers also have a dishonest woman or favorite servant who actually runs the country."

One day, while chatting, my master paid me a compliment I did not deserve. He was sure I had been born into the upper class because I was so superior in shape, color, and cleanliness to the yahoos of his nation. In addition, not only could I speak, but I could also reason, after a fashion.

I humbly thanked his honor, while assuring him, "I was born of plain honest parents, who were barely able to give me a decent education. Nobility, among us, is not what you imagine. Our young noblemen are bred from childhood to do nothing and live luxuriously. As soon as they are old enough, they waste their health on pleasure and contract terrible diseases from wicked women. When their fortunes are almost spent, they marry women who are unhealthy and disagreeable but very wealthy, usually women they despise. Their children are, more often than not, corrupt, weak, or deformed. Such families seldom last more than three generations unless the wife finds someone healthy—a neighbor or servant—to father her children.

"The true marks of nobility are a weak body, a thin face, and a pale complexion. If a nobleman looks too healthy, people assume his father is the carriage driver. Weak minds are as common among nobles as ill health. Their thinking, such as it is, is driven by ignorance, lust, and pride.

"Master, keep in mind that the permission of these nobles is required to pass or change any law. In addition, they have the power to decide all matters of property. And those whom they judge have no right of repeal."

PART III
Chapter 7

The reader may wonder why I gave my master such an honest evaluation of the human race. After all, he was likely to have the lowest possible opinion of the human race due to our similarity to yahoos. The reason is plain. I had been strongly influenced by the Houyhnhnms. They were so admirable that I began to see the human race in a different light. I no longer felt I had to defend the honor of my own kind. My master was so wise and such a good judge of character that he recognized immediately the thousands of flaws in my species and in me.

I had also come to detest falsehood. I was determined to be completely honest at all cost. Further, after one year in the country of the Houyhnhnms, I had come to idolize its inhabitants. I made up my mind never to return to humankind. I would spend the rest of my days here. Alas, it was not my destiny to do so. I take some comfort in knowing that I always put the best possible face on the faults of my countrymen. Indeed, isn't every man partial to the place of his birth?

I had answered all of my master's questions. His curiosity seemed fully satisfied.

Early one morning, he commanded me to sit close to him (an honor he had never before granted). He said, "I have thought deeply about your story. I consider yours a species of animal with a tiny amount of reasoning ability. Unfortunately, you make little use of the intelligence you have except for corrupt purposes. Your needs are so great, you spend a lifetime trying to satisfy them. But you do not succeed.

"You lack the strength and agility of a common yahoo. You walk—unsteadily—on only one pair of feet. You make your claws useless for defense. You remove the hair from your chin, exposing your face to the sun and the weather. You cannot run or climb trees as well as the yahoos of our country.

"The problems with your government and laws stem from the weakness in your ability to reason. You have no right to claim true intelligence. Your own story proves that, even though I can tell you hid many details and often said the thing which was not.

"I am more convinced than ever that I am correct. Even you agree that you are exactly like a yahoo physically, except where you are inferior. Now I know you are even more like a yahoo than I previously understood.

"Yahoos hate one another more than they hate any other species of animal. At one time it was thought this was because yahoos could see how revolting the bodies of their fellows looked, though they could not see the same in themselves. That might explain why your species of yahoo invented clothing, to conceal your deformities. But your clothing does nothing to stop your dreadful behavior.

"If we were to give five yahoos enough food for fifty, they would, instead of eating peacefully, immediately begin fighting among themselves.

"Sometimes a cow dies and time passes before a Houyhnhnm can claim it for his own yahoos. Herds of nearby yahoos come and battle for the carcass. They inflict terrible wounds, though they rarely kill one another. Fortunately, they have not yet invented instruments of death like those you possess. Yahoos from nearby neighborhoods often fight each other for no reason in particular. Those in the herd that loses often return home and engage in what you called a civil war.

"In some parts of our country, yahoos have found certain shining stones of several colors. Yahoos have become violently fond of these stones. They will dig for days to get some, carry away what they find, and hide them in piles in their kennels. I could never discover the reason for this unnatural desire for stones, but it seems to relate to the greed of mankind that you have described. Once, as an experiment, I secretly removed one yahoo's stockpile of stones. Soon after, he missed his treasure and began howling miserably. Next, he started biting and hitting the members of his herd. Finally, he began to get very weak, unable to eat, sleep, or work. When my master ordered a servant to secretly return the stones, the yahoo quickly recovered. He also took great care to remove his stones to a better hiding place. Since then he has been an unusually agreeable brute.

"It is common, when two yahoos quarrel over a stone in a field, for a third yahoo to take advantage, and carry it away for himself. This practice reminds me of your description of lawsuits."

In fact, I thought the outcome in his example superior to what happens in our courts. In his example, the quarreling yahoos only lost the stone they each hoped to get. In England, the case would have dragged on until both defendants lost everything they already owned. Then the judge would have dismissed the case.

Yahoos will eat almost anything. My master considered this indiscriminate appetite of the yahoos their most vile quality. They devour everything in their way: herbs, roots, berries, the decayed flesh of animals. They prefer the food they steal to the food their masters provide. As long as the food holds out, they eat. When yahoos feel ready to burst, they use a certain root that empties the system. Then they continue to stuff themselves.

Yahoos also make use of very juicy, but rare, root. They seek it eagerly. It produces the same effects that wine has on us. Sometimes they hug and sometimes tear one another apart. They howl, grin, chatter, tumble, and then fall asleep in the mud.

I had already noticed that yahoos were the only animals in this country subject to any disease. The language of the Houyhnhnms has no specific word for their illnesses. Rather, they are all called *hnea-yahoo*, in English, "yahoo's evil." The cure is a mixture of dung and urine, forced down the sick yahoo's throat. I have seen this mixture used successfully. Therefore, I freely recommend it to my countrymen as a cure for all diseases produced by overindulging.

"As far as learning, government, art, industry, and such things," my master confessed, "I find little or no resemblance between the yahoos of my country and those in yours. But I am only comparing basic natures." My master then began to discuss certain characteristics of yahoos. I had never mentioned them, but he suspected humans shared these qualities.

"I have heard some Houyhnhnms say there is a ruling yahoo in most herds. He can be identified easily. He is always more deformed and more evil than the rest. This leader usually has an assistant, a yahoo as much like himself as possible. The assistant's job is to lick his master's feet and buttocks. He is also responsible for driving female yahoos to the leader's kennel. For his services, the assistant sometimes receives a piece of jackass flesh. This favorite is hated by the rest of the herd, and therefore, can always be found near the leader. The assistant keeps his job until someone worse can be found. How closely this compares to your royal courts, favorites, and ministers of state, you will have to decide for yourself."

My master also told me, "Yahoos have other strange qualities. Yahoo males will quarrel and fight with females as fiercely as with each other. Also, yahoos have a unique love of nastiness and dirt. Every other animal has a natural love of cleanliness." I was glad I did not have to defend mankind from the first accusation. But, I could have offered a good defense to the second. Had there been pigs in the land of the Houyhnhnms, I would have shown my master that he had been wrong to put humans in a class by themselves when it comes to dirt.

My master continued. "Sometimes a yahoo will slink into a corner, lie down, howl, and force away anyone who comes near. The only cure we have ever found was a steady routine of hard work." I gladly remained silent once again, to save my species embarrassment. Indeed, I have seen the same behavior in lazy, rich, spoiled humans. Some call it "spleen." I have always felt hard work would be an effective cure.

His honor had more such comments. "We have noticed that a female yahoo will often stare secretly at young males passing by. She will alternate between showing herself and continuing to hide. When she can be seen, she makes peculiar gestures and strange faces. At the same time, she gives off a most offensive odor. When a male approaches, she slowly walks away, looking back the whole time. Then she goes to some convenient place where she knows the male will find her.

"When a strange female appears the first time, three or four other female yahoos will stare, chatter, smile, and smell her all over. Then they turn away, making faces that show their contempt." The crudeness, flirtatiousness, and cattiness he described are common among females of my country. I was saddened to think that such behavior might be a natural, universal instinct. I also expected my master to accuse yahoos of the various perversions so common among English men and women. But these behaviors may not be natural after all. They must be the product of civilization.

I was intrigued by the many similarities between yahoos and Englishmen. I wanted to study yahoos more closely, to see if I could learn more. Therefore, I often asked his honor to let me mingle with the local yahoo herds. He always gave his permission, convinced my natural hatred of yahoos would keep me from being corrupted by them. To be safe, he ordered one of his servants to be my guard. Without protection I would not have dared to conduct my experiments.

I have reason to believe yahoos considered me one of them. To further that impression I would remove the clothing from my arms and chest. Then, some yahoos were sure to approach me. Like monkeys, they would imitate everything I did. But they also showed signs that they disliked me because I was more civilized.

Yahoos are amazingly agile, even as children.

Once, however, I was able to catch a young male of three years old. I treated it as tenderly as possible to see how it would react. The little rascal started screaming, scratching, and biting so violently I was forced to let it go. A number of yahoos, hearing his cries, approached. When they saw the child had escaped and that I was guarded, they left me alone. I did notice that the young animal's flesh smelled terribly, somewhere between the smell of a weasel and a fox, but much more disagreeable. I forgot to mention (and perhaps the reader might wish I had continued to forget) that while I held the disgusting toddler, it left a yellow liquid all over my clothes. Fortunately, there was a stream nearby.

Yahoos can be trained to lift heavy objects and carry loads. The Houyhnhnms keep yahoos they need in huts close to their houses. They send the rest to certain fields. There, they dig up roots, eat herbs, search for dead animals to eat, and sometimes catch weasels and *luhimuhs* (a sort of wild rat), which they greedily devour.

One very hot day, I decided to bathe in a nearby river. I stripped myself stark naked and went into the stream. A young female yahoo standing nearby saw me and leaped into the water within five yards of me. She immediately locked me in an over-enthusiastic embrace. I roared as loudly as I could, and my guard came galloping. She let go reluctantly and climbed up the opposite bank, where she stood gazing and howling the entire time I was putting on my clothes. The re-telling of this incident entertained my master and his family but humiliated me. I had to admit that I was a real yahoo, since the females desired me as one of their own species.

I lived three years in the country of the Houyhnhnms. Readers of travel books like this expect to read about the manners and customs of the people the author encounters. Indeed, the desire to learn about other cultures was one of the reasons for my travels.

These noble Houyhnhnms are extremely virtuous by nature. They do not understand how any creature with intelligence can be evil. Their focus in life is to fully develop the ability to reason and to be completely controlled by it. Their thinking is never clouded by emotions or personal gain. Therefore, they have firm convictions about what is right and what is wrong and never need to argue the different sides of an issue. Houyhnhnms consider investigating the physical universe a waste of time. Moral principles are the proper subject for study. I had great difficulty helping my master understand the word "opinion." He had no concept of how any point could ever be disputed. He believed that if reason did not lead to one undeniable answer, the resulting uncertainty ruled out having an opinion. Disagreement is an evil unknown to Houyhnhnms.

Friendship and kindness are the two principal virtues of Houyhnhnms. Among them, a stranger is treated the same as a close friend. Wherever a Houyhnhnm goes he can feel at home. Houyhnhnms behave courteously at all times, but never waste time on formalities. Reason, not love, dictates how they care for and educate their offspring. I have witnessed my master showing the same affection to his neighbor's children that he shows to his own. They believe it is only natural for one Houyhnhnm to love all Houyhnhnms.

After an adult female has produced one offspring of each sex, she no longer has intimate contact with the father. Only in the rare case of the death of a child do they resume relations. Should a couple past the age of childbearing lose an offspring, a younger couple gives them one of their colts. The younger couple then conceives another child. Inferior Houyhnhnms, bred to be servants, are allowed to produce three of each sex, to be servants in the noble families.

Houyhnhnms choose mates by colors with the goal of producing an agreeable mixture. Strength is the most valued characteristic in a male, beauty in the female. Mates are chosen not for love but to preserve the quality of the race. If a female happens to excel in strength, a handsome mate is chosen.

Courtship, love, presents, and property settlements do not exist in the land of the Houyhnhnms. These terms cannot be expressed in their language. Here, young couples meet and are joined because parents and friends wish it. Violation of marriage and other immoral acts never occur. The married pair pass their lives in friendship and mutual goodwill, the same goodwill they bear to all others of their species.

Their method for educating the youth of both sexes deserves imitation. The young rarely taste oats or milk before they are eighteen years old. In summer they and their parents graze two hours in the morning and two in the evening. But servants graze half as long; some of their grass is brought home so they can eat it at times when they can best be spared from their work.

Both sexes learn self-control, hard work, exercise, and cleanliness. My master thought it monstrous to give females a different kind of education from males, except for some training in home economics. As he wisely observed, half of England's natives are only good for bringing children into the world. Trusting the care of children to such useless animals, he said, was a tragedy.

The Houyhnhnms train their youth in strength, speed, and endurance. Exercise consists of racing up and down steep hills and over hard stony ground. When they are all in a sweat, they are ordered to leap into a pond or river. Four times a year the youth in each district meet to prove their skill in running and leaping and other feats of strength and agility. The winner is rewarded with a song in his or her praise. At this festival, the servants drive into the field a herd of yahoos loaded with hay, oats, and milk for the Houyhnhnms. Then the brutes are immediately driven back, to avoid offending those in attendance.

Every fourth year, on the day spring arrives, representatives from the entire nation meet together in a field about twenty miles from our house. The meeting lasts five or six days. The representatives discuss the condition of the various districts. They discuss the supply of hay, oats, cows, and yahoos. Supplies are immediately delivered to locales lacking anything (which rarely happens). Matters concerning the raising of children are also settled at this meeting. For example, if a Houyhnhnm has two male offspring, he exchanges one with a Houyhnhnm who has two females.

Chapter 9

One of these general assemblies was held about three months before my departure. My master went as the representative of our district. Upon returning, he gave me a very specific report on what had happened. In this council an old debate had been resumed. The question was, "Should yahoos be exterminated from the face of the earth?"

One member in favor of extermination argued that, "Yahoos are the most filthy, offensive, and deformed animals nature ever produced. They are impatient, lazy, mischievous, and wicked. They would secretly drink milk from our cows, kill and devour our cats, and trample down the oats and grass if they were not watched every minute." He reminded the assembly of the widely held belief that yahoos had not always been in their country. Rather, long ago the first two yahoos appeared together on a mountain. They multiplied so quickly that they threatened to overrun the entire nation. The Houyhnhnms, to get rid of this evil, hunted the yahoos. They rounded up and fenced in the entire herd. They destroyed all adult yahoos. Every Houyhnhnm kept two young yahoos in a kennel and tamed them for use in carrying loads and hauling carriages.

The theory that yahoos were not native seemed to be supported by the violent hatred the Houyhnhnms—and other animals—had for them. The representative calling for the elimination of yahoos suggested jackasses as a practical substitute. "Asses," he said, "are handsome animals, easily maintained, naturally tame, relatively lacking in offensive smell, and strong enough for work. Jackasses may be inferior in agility and rather loud, but I prefer their braying to the horrible howling of the yahoos."

Several others agreed. My master proposed a compromise. He agreed with the traditional story about the first two yahoos. "I have more reason than ever to believe the old tale. I have now in my possession a certain wonderful yahoo of whom most of you have heard and many seen." He told how he first found me. He described my artificial covering made of the skins and hairs of other animals.

"This yahoo speaks his own language and has thoroughly learned ours. He described for me in detail his country where yahoos govern and

Houyhnhnms serve. I have seen this yahoo without his covering. He has all the qualities of a yahoo born with a touch of reason, though far inferior to the Houyhnhnm race. This yahoo told of a custom in his country of castrating young Houyhnhnms. This makes them tame. The operation is easy and safe. I suggest we try castration with our younger yahoos here. It should make them fitter for our use. But, more importantly, it will eventually put an end to the whole species, without killing. In the meantime, we can breed jackasses, which have the further advantage of being fit for service at five years old. Yahoos, as you know, are not fit until twelve."

My master related many such details about the meeting, but he kept secret some information that related to me. I would find out about it soon enough, and unhappily, as the reader will learn.

Houyhnhnms have no form of writing. As a result, all of their knowledge is passed from generation to generation orally. Their history is rather uneventful since they are a united and highly moral people, cut off from other nations. I have already observed that they are subject to no diseases and therefore have no need of physicians. However, they use excellent herbal medicines to cure accidental bruises and cuts.

Houyhnhnms base their year on the revolution of the sun and moon, but do not use weeks. They understand the motions of the sun and moon and the cause of eclipses. Their knowledge of the heavens stops there however.

The poetry of the Houyhnhnms is the finest in the world. They have special skill in the use of similes. The beauty and detail in their descriptions are unmatched. Poems treat such subjects as friendship and praise for the winners of races.

Their buildings, though quite simple in design, are well constructed. They offer excellent protection from the cold and heat. Houses are constructed from wood. A certain tree common to their forests dies at about forty and soon falls. Its wood is straight and strong. With sharp stones, the Houyhnhnms sharpen one end of each piece and stick it in the ground. These are placed about ten inches apart. Straw and branches are woven between them. The roof is made in the same way, and so are the doors.

The Houyhnhnms are more skillful in using their hooves than I ever imagined possible. I gave a white mare in our family a needle, and she was able to thread it. Houyhnhnms milk cows, reap oats, and do all the work for which we use our hands. With a kind of hard flint, they grind other stones into wedges, axes, and hammers. With tools made of flint, they cut their hay and reap their oats. Yahoos haul the harvest to covered huts where servants separate the grain for storage. Houyhnhnms make pots from wood and sun-baked clay.

Except in cases of accident, Houyhnhnms die only of old age. They are buried in hard to find places. Their friends and relatives express neither joy nor grief at their departure. The dying have no regrets about leaving the world. They regard death as little more than a return home after a visit to a neighbor. Once, my master had invited a friend and his family to come to his house. The wife and children of his friend came very late. She made two apologies. First, she excused her husband, who, as she said, happened that very morning to *shnuwnh*. The word, full of significance in their language, is not easily translated into English. Literally, it means, "to retire to your first mother." She also explained that her husband had died late that morning. She had spent a long time consulting with her servants about a convenient place for burying the body. I noted to myself at the time that the recent widow behaved as cheerfully as ever that day. She died about three months later.

Houyhnhnms live seventy to seventy-five years, and sometimes—though rarely—to eighty. Starting a few weeks before death, they gradually waste away but feel no pain. During this time friends often visit, because the dying cannot easily go out. However, about ten days before death— their ability to know the right time is amazing— they return the visits of their nearest neighbors carried in a kind of sled drawn by yahoos. They bid a sincere farewell to their friends, as if they are going to some distant part of the country where they will spend the rest of their lives.

The only words Houyhnhnms have to express anything negative are the terms they use to describe yahoos. They create expressions for the foolishness of a servant, the misbehavior of a child, a stone that cuts the feet, bad weather, and similar matters by adding *yahoo* to an existing word. For instance, the term for a poorly built house is *ynholmhnmrohlnw yahoo*.

I could tell much more about the lives and virtues of this excellent people. When I publish my upcoming book on Houyhnhnms, interested readers should consult it. For now, I will relate the story of the catastrophe I suffered.

PART III
Chapter 10

In time, my life with the Houyhnhnms became quite comfortable. My master ordered a room made for me about six yards from the house. I plastered the sides and floors with clay and wove mats from rushes to serve as carpets. I made pillow covers from hemp—which grows wild there—and filled them with feathers. With traps made from yahoo hair, I had captured birds that were excellent food. I constructed two chairs with my knife. I made new clothing for myself from the skins of rabbits and another beautiful animal about the same size, called *nnuhnoh*. From them, I also made stockings. I soled my shoes with wood and replaced the leather with the skins of yahoos dried in the sun. I often got honey out of hollow trees, which I mixed with water and ate with my bread.

In the land of the Houyhnhnms, I enjoyed perfect health and peace of mind. I never had to endure the disloyalty of a friend or the insults of an enemy. I felt no pressure to bribe, flatter, or grovel before a great man. There were no physicians to destroy your body, lawyers to bankrupt you, or paid informers to make false accusations. Here were no backbiters, pickpockets, attorneys, buffoons, politicians, murderers, robbers, or followers of political parties. No jails or whipping-posts. No cheating shopkeepers or mechanics, no bullies, no drunkards. No expensive wives. No ignorant scholars. No lords, fiddlers, judges, or dancing teachers.

I had the good fortune, several times, to be present for conversations between my master and Houyhnhnms who came to visit or dine. Often, both he and his company would ask me questions and graciously welcome my answers. Sometimes I had the honor of accompanying my master when he paid visits. I never spoke on such occasions, except to answer a question. I did so with regret, because I would rather have listened to them. Every word spoken between Houyhnhnms was educational for me. Every conversation I overheard meant a chance to learn something that would make me a better man. Each exchange was courteous, though these discussions had no leader and no rules. There were no interruptions, angry outbursts, or differences of opinion.

Houyhnhnms believe that short silences improve conversation. I found this to be true.

During those little pauses, the participants would develop new ideas. Their favorite subjects were friendship and kindness, orderliness and thrift, the nature of virtue, how best to use the power to reason, or some decision to be made at the next great assembly. They also loved to discuss the qualities of fine poetry. I may add, without bragging, that my presence often provided a subject. My master would inform his friends about my life story and my country. Those in attendance had many comments about mankind, most of them unfavorable. For that reason, I shall not repeat what they said. I can say, however, that my master understood yahoos much better than I did. He could list all our vices and follies, including those I had never mentioned to him. He would always conclude, "How vile, as well as miserable, such a creature must be."

I freely admit that the small amount of worthwhile knowledge I have, I learned from my master's instruction and the discussions he had with his friends. I would more willingly listen to them than rule the greatest and wisest assembly in Europe. I admired the strength, beauty, and speed of the Houyhnhnms. Who could not help but revere a creature so magnificent yet so gentle? These feelings merged with the gratitude I felt. I welcomed their willingness to differentiate me from the others of my species, those revolting yahoos.

I began to realize that my family, my friends, my countrymen, indeed the entire human race are nothing more than yahoos, though a bit more civilized and well-spoken. Whenever I would see myself in a Houyhnhnm lake or fountain, I would turn away in horror. I had grown to hate myself. After spending so much time with Houyhnhnms, I began to imitate their gestures and their way of walking. Now my friends often tell me bluntly, "You trot like a horse." I consider that a great compliment. When I speak, I sometimes take on the voice and mannerism of the Houyhnhnms. When I hear myself ridiculed for that, I am not bothered in the least.

In the midst of all my happiness, when I believed myself settled for life, my master sent for me, a little earlier than usual. I could tell immediately he was at a loss how to begin. After a short silence, he told me, "I do not know how you will take what I am about to say. At the last general assembly, when the fate of the yahoos was discussed, many representatives objected to my treating a yahoo, you, more like a Houyhnhnm than a brute animal. It is well known that I frequently converse with you, learning and taking pleasure in your company. They believe this defies the laws of nature and reason. I was commanded either to treat you the way we treat the rest of our yahoos or to order you to swim back to the place from which you came. Every Houyhnhnm who has ever seen you warned against putting you with the other yahoos. They believe your ability to reason, though quite basic, could be dangerous. Yahoos are thieves with big appetites. You might lead other yahoos into hiding, bringing them out at night to feed off our cattle."

My master added, "Every day, the local Houyhnhnms demand I obey the assembly's order. I cannot put it off much longer. I doubt you can swim to another country. I wish you could construct some vehicle, such as those you often have described to me, to carry you on the sea. My servants can assist you." He concluded, "As for me, I would have been happy to keep you in my service for as long as you lived. You have cured yourself of many bad habits by attempting, as much as your inferior nature allows, to imitate Houyhnhnms."

I should mention that an order of the Houyhnhnm general assembly is called an "urgent request." No rational creature needs to be ordered to do something. To them, no rational creature can disobey reason. In a reasonable amount of time, I would be expected to undertake this challenge.

I was struck with grief and despair at hearing my master's words. I fainted at his feet. When I came to myself, he told me, "I thought you were dead." Houyhnhnms do not faint.

I answered weakly, "Death would have been

too great a happiness for me. Reason should have led your assembly to another conclusion. I could never swim from here to another country. You lack the materials necessary for making a small boat. I want to obey, but the order is impossible to carry out. Therefore I consider myself condemned to death. But that is the least of my problems. If, through some amazing good fortune I would escape here alive, how could I ever bear to pass my days among yahoos? I might become corrupt once again." But I knew the decision of the assembly would not change and that I must obey. Therefore, I humbly accepted the offer of his servants' assistance. I declared that, given a reasonable amount of time, I would undertake this challenge and attempt to keep myself alive. Should I ever return to England, I pledged to celebrate Houyhnhnms and help mankind learn from their example.

My master replied graciously. He gave me two months to finish my boat. He ordered the servant who had been my guard to assist me. Together, we went to that part of the coast where my rebellious crew had left me. From a high vantage point and using my pocket telescope, I could clearly see an island about fifteen miles away. I decided it would be the first place I would go. Beyond that, I left my fortune to fate.

We returned home and got to work immediately. But I shall not trouble the reader with a detailed description of what we did. Suffice to say, that in six weeks time (and with the help of my guard, who did the most difficult work) I finished a sort of Indian canoe, though much larger. I covered it with yahoo skins stitched together with hemp. My sail was composed of skins of the same animal. However, for this purpose I made use of the youngest yahoos I could get. The skin of older yahoos would have been too tough and too thick. I also made four paddles. I stocked myself with the boiled flesh of rabbits and fowls and took two containers, one filled with milk and the other with water.

I tested my canoe in a large pond, near my master's house. Then I corrected anything that hadn't worked properly. I used tallow boiled down from the fat of yahoos to fill the cracks until the boat was watertight. When I was done, I had it drawn to the seaside, under the supervision of my guard and another servant.

When all was ready, the day came for my departure. I said goodbye to my master and lady and the whole family. My eyes filled with tears. My heart nearly sank with grief. His honor, out of curiosity, and perhaps (if I may say so myself) partly out of kindness, was determined to see me depart in my canoe. He even invited several of his neighbors to accompany him. I was forced to wait more than an hour for a favorable tide. Fortunately, the wind was blowing toward the

island to which I intended to steer. I bid farewell to my master a second time. When I bent down to kiss his hoof, he did me the honor of raising it gently to my mouth.

I know how much I have been criticized for including this last detail. My detractors wonder how a person as illustrious as me could ever sink so low in servitude to an inferior being. Most travel writers boast about the attentions they have received, not those they have given. If these critics learned more about the noble Houyhnhnms, they would soon change their opinion.

I paid my respects to everyone who accompanied my master. Getting into my canoe, I pushed off from shore.

Chapter 11

I began this desperate voyage on February 15, 1715, at nine o'clock in the morning. Though the wind was favorable, I only used the paddles at first. Realizing I would soon tire, I set up my little sail. With that and the help of the tide, I went almost five miles an hour, as near as I can guess. My master and his friends remained on the shore until I was almost out of sight. I often heard my friend the guard crying out, "*Hnuy illa nyha, majah yahoo*," which means, "Take care of yourself, gentle yahoo."

My plan was to find a small, uninhabited island that could, with enough work, supply my basic needs. I would have been happier there than if I were the prime minister of the most civilized royal court in Europe. I could not bear the thought of living once again in a land governed by yahoos. In complete isolation I would at least be alone with my thoughts. I could spend my day contemplating the virtues of those superior Houyhnhnms, without any opportunity to be corrupted by my own species.

If you recall, during the mutiny against me I had been confined to my cabin. From what little I could gather from overhearing the sailors, I had guessed, at that time, that we were 10 degrees south of the Cape of Good Hope. Although this was only an educated guess, I decided to steer my course eastward, hoping to reach the southwest coast of New Holland. The wind was blowing steadily to the west. By six in the evening I calculated I had gone eastward nearly sixty miles. I spied a very small island and spent the night there. It was little more than a rock with one stream. From there, I could plainly see land to the east. Starting early in the morning, I arrived on New Holland in seven hours.

I saw no inhabitants where I landed. Being unarmed, I was afraid to venture inland. I found some shellfish on the shore and ate them raw, not daring to start a fire. After finding an excellent stream with fresh water, I rested there for three days.

On the fourth day, I dared to explore a little too far inland. I spotted twenty or thirty natives on a hill not five hundred yards away. They were stark naked—men, women, and children, standing around a fire. One of them spied me and alerted the rest. Five came in my direction. Moving as quickly as I could, I reached my canoe and shoved off. The savages were able to shoot some arrows at me before I got too far from shore. One wounded me deeply on the inside of my left knee. I shall carry the scar to my grave. Thinking the arrow might be poisoned, I paddled out of reach of their arrows and sucked out the wound. Then I bandaged it as best I could.

At a loss what to do, I steered towards the north. I was forced to paddle because the wind, though gentle, was against me. Suddenly, I saw a sail to the north getting closer by the minute. I was in some doubt over what to do. But, in the end, my hatred of yahoos got the better of me, and I turned around. I was willing to trust my fate to the same barbarians I had escaped in the morning rather than live with European yahoos. I left my canoe as close as I could to the shore and hid behind a stone by the little brook with the excellent water.

The ship came within a mile or so. The captain sent out one of the longboats to collect fresh water. I did not notice the boat until it was almost on shore. It was too late to look for another hiding place. The seamen saw my canoe when they landed. They knew its owner could not be far off. Four of them, well armed, searched until they found me flat on my face behind the stone. They stared at my strange clothing: my coat made of skins, my wooden-soled shoes, and my furry stock-ings. They knew immediately I was not one of the natives, who all go naked. One of the seamen, in Portuguese, told me to get up. Then he asked who I was. I understand Portuguese. Getting up on my feet, I said, "I am a poor yahoo banished from the Houyhnhnms. Please let me go." They were amazed to hear me answer in their own language. However, they could not understand all my talk about yahoos and Houyhnhnms. They also could not help but laugh at the strange way I spoke, which resembled the neighing of a horse. I trem-bled, filled with fear and hatred. I again asked per-mission to depart. I started to slowly move toward my canoe, but they grabbed me. They wanted to know more. "What country are you from? What are you doing here?" they asked, among other things.

I answered, "I was born in England, which I left about five years ago. At that time, our coun-tries were at peace. Please do not treat me as an enemy. I mean you no harm. I'm just a poor yahoo seeking a deserted place to spend the rest of his miserable life."

When they began to talk, I thought I had never heard or seen anything more unnatural. It was as if a dog or cow in England started speaking, or a yahoo in Houyhnhnmland. The Portuguese were equally amazed at my strange clothing and odd manner of pronouncing my words, which, however, they understood very well. They spoke to me with sympathy and said, "The captain will surely carry you to Lisbon for free. From there you can return to your own country. Two of us will go back to the ship, inform the captain of what we have seen, and wait for his orders. In the meantime, unless you give your solemn oath not to run away, we will have to tie you up." I thought it best to comply with their proposal. They were very curious to know my story, but I gave them very little satisfaction. They assumed that my misfortunes had made me mad. In two hours, the boat, which had already delivered the fresh water, returned with the captain's command to bring me on board. I begged for freedom, but to no avail. The men tied me and threw me in the boat. I was taken to the ship and then to the captain's cabin.

His name was Pedro de Mendez, a very courteous and generous person. He requested I give some account of myself. He offered me something to eat or drink. He promised, "You shall be treated as I would expect to be treated in similar circumstances." I was surprised to find such courtesy in a yahoo. However, I remained silent and angry, ready to faint at the very smell of him and his men. At last I asked for something to eat out of my own canoe. Instead, he ordered a chicken and some excellent wine. Then he ordered that I be put to bed in a very clean cabin. I would not undress myself and just lay on the bedclothes. In half an hour, I snuck out, thinking the crew was at dinner. I made it to the side of the ship, intending to leap into the sea and swim for my life rather than continue among yahoos. But one of the seamen prevented me from jumping and informed the captain. I was chained inside my cabin.

After dinner Don Pedro came to me and wanted to know the reason behind my desperate attempt at escape. "I assure you,' he said, "I want to do everything I can to help you." He spoke so movingly, that at last I decided to treat him like an animal with some small reasoning ability.

I gave him a very short summary of my voyage: the conspiracy against me; the country where they marooned me; and my five years there. He regarded everything I said as if it were a dream or a vision. I took great offense at that. I had completely lost the ability to lie, a special talent among yahoos no matter where they reside. As a result, they suspect the truth to be a lie when spoken by others of their own species. I asked him, "Is it the custom in your country to say the thing which was not?" I assured him, "I have almost forgotten what a falsehood is. I could have lived a thousand years in Houyhnhnmland and never heard a lie from the humblest servant. I do not care if you believe me or not. However, in return for your kind treatment and because I know it is the nature of your species to be corrupt, I will give you the benefit of the doubt. I am prepared to address any reservations you have about my story. In the end, you will recognize I am telling the truth."

The captain, a wise man, after many attempts to trip me up in some part of my story, at last began to have a better opinion of my honesty. But he added, "Since you profess such a strong attachment to truth, you must give your word of honor not to make any attempt on your own life. Otherwise, I must keep you prisoner until we arrive in Lisbon." I gave him the promise he required. At the same time I protested, "I would rather suffer the greatest hardships than return to live among yahoos."

Our voyage passed without incident. In gratitude to the captain, I sometimes sat with him at his request, concealing my distaste for humankind. When it sometimes slipped out, he let it pass without comment. Most of the day I confined myself to my cabin to avoid seeing any of the crew. The captain often asked me to strip off my primitive clothing. To replace it, he offered to lend me the best suit of clothes he had. This I would not accept, detesting the thought of covering myself with anything that had been on the back of a yahoo. I only asked him to lend me two clean shirts. I believed they would not contaminate me very much since they had been washed. These I changed every second day, washing them myself.

We arrived at Lisbon November 5th, 1715. When we landed, the captain helped me cover myself with his cape to prevent anyone from seeing me. He brought me to his house and, at my request, led me to the highest room in the back. I asked him, "Please keep secret everything I told you about the Houyhnhnms. If even a hint of the story gets out, not only will people flock to see me, but I will be at risk of imprisonment." The captain persuaded me to accept a new suit of clothes, though I would not allow the tailor to measure me. Fortunately, Don Pedro is almost my size, and everything fit me well enough. He equipped me with other necessities, all new. Still, I aired everything out for twenty-four hours.

The captain had no wife and only three servants, none of whom attended him at mealtime. His manner was very friendly. That, combined with his wisdom, made him quite tolerable company. He eventually gained my confidence enough that I dared to look out the back window. Little by little, he convinced me to venture into another room. From there, I peeped into the street, but I drew my head back in fright. In a week's time he got me down to the door. My terror gradually lessened, but my hatred and contempt seemed to increase. At last, I became brave enough to walk the street in his company though I stopped up my nose with sweet smelling herbs.

In ten days, Don Pedro, whom I had told a bit about my home life, told me it was a matter of honor that I return to my native country to live with my wife and children. He told me of an English ship in port just ready to sail. He promised to supply me with everything I needed. It would be boring to repeat our arguments on the subject. Finally, he convinced me by insisting, "You will never find the secluded island you dream about, but you might be able to insist on solitude in your own home."

I agreed at last, realizing it was the best I could do. I left Lisbon the 24th day of November, in an English merchant ship. Don Pedro accompanied me to the dock, and lent me some money. He bid a fond farewell and embraced me, which I stomached as well as I could. During this voyage I had no dealings with the captain or any of his crew. Pretending I was sick, I kept to my cabin. On the 5th of December at about nine in the morning we landed. By three that afternoon I arrived safely at my house in Redriff.

My wife and family greeted me with surprise and joy because they had been sure I was dead. I must confess, however, that the sight of them filled me with hatred and disgust. My revulsion was even stronger when I considered how closely we were related. Since my unfortunate expulsion from the Houyhnhnm country, I had forced myself to tolerate the sight of yahoos. But my memory was filled with the virtues and ideas of those glorious Houyhnhnms. When I realized that, by having sexual intercourse with one yahoo,

I had increased the species, I was terribly ashamed, confused, and horrified. As soon as I entered the house, my wife took me in her arms and kissed me. I was so unaccustomed to the touch of that repulsive animal that I fell into a faint.

As I write this, it has been five years since my return. During the first year, I could not endure having my wife or children in my presence, much less eating with them. Their very smell was unbearable. To this day, they dare not even touch my food, or drink out of the same cup. I am still unable to let one of them take me by the hand. The first money I spent was for two young stallions. Next to them, my favorite person is the groom who cares for them. I love the smell he takes on from being in the stable. My horses understand me fairly well. I talk to them at least four hours every day. They will never know bridle or saddle. They live in great harmony with me and friendship with each other.

Chapter 12

Gentle reader, I have given you an accurate history of my travels for sixteen years and over seven months. In it, I have been more painstaking about reporting the truth than I have been in embellishing my tale. I could, like other travel writers, have astonished you with strange improbable tales. I chose instead to tell my story plainly and in the simplest style. My principal goal was to inform, not to amuse.

It is easy for those who travel to remote countries seldom visited by Englishmen to invent descriptions of wonderful animals both at sea and on land. A travel writer's chief aim should be to make men wiser and better, to improve their minds by pointing out the bad as well as the good things they discover in foreign places.

I heartily wish a law would be passed requiring every travel writer—before being permitted to publish an account of his voyages—to take a solemn oath that his work is absolutely true to the best of his knowledge. Then writers will no longer be able to deceive unsuspecting readers with outrageous fantasies in an attempt to sell more books. When I was younger, I read several travel books with great delight. But once I had voyaged around the globe, I became disgusted to learn my innocence had been abused. Much of what I had read was contradicted by what I saw. Now, some of my acquaintances believe the story of my humble undertaking will be of interest to the people of England. Therefore, I have imposed a strict rule on myself. I will adhere to the truth. I am never even tempted to stray from this principle as long as I recall the example of my noble master and the other remarkable Houyhnhnms.

As the saying goes, no one earns a reputation as a great author from writing that requires neither genius nor learning. Travel writers need no special talent other than a good memory or an accurate journal. I know likewise that a travel book is quickly forgotten as soon as the next such account is published. It is highly probable that travelers who visit the countries I described will, by detecting my errors (if there be any) and adding new discoveries of their own, make the world forget that I was ever an author. This indeed would be too great a humiliation, if I wrote for fame. Since my only purpose is the public good, I can never be completely disappointed. Who can read about the virtues of the glorious Houyhnhnms, without being ashamed of his own vices? Wouldn't we be better off if we paid attention to the morality and government of the Brobdingnagians? But I will refrain from further comment, letting my wise readers come to their own conclusions.

I am pleased that this work of mine is beyond criticism. How can anyone object to a writer who sticks to the facts? How can anyone be offended by an account of events in distant countries where we have no economic interests? I have carefully avoided all the shortcomings of common writers of travels. Besides, I write without prejudice or ill will against any man or group. I write for the noblest reason, to inform and instruct mankind. I can do so because, in complete humility, I can claim some degree of superiority. For years, I lived with and learned from the most accomplished Houyhnhnms. I write without expecting any profit or praise. I never put down a single word that may cause anyone to take offense, even those who are most ready to take offense. I am fully justified in declaring myself an author who is completely blameless.

I confess that some people told me it was my duty, as soon as I returned, to give the Minister of Foreign Affairs a complete account of my journey. After all, they claimed, whatever lands are discovered by an Englishman belong to the crown. But I doubt we could conquer the countries I visited as easily as Ferdinando Cortez triumphed over the naked Americans. The Lilliputians, I think, are hardly worth the expense involved in sending a fleet and army. I question whether it would be sensible or safe to attempt to conquer the Brobdingnagians. The Houyhnhnms appear unprepared for war, especially the use of long-range weapons. However, if I were Minister of State, I would advise against invading them. Their caution, unity, fearlessness, and love of country would amply compensate for all the defects in their military. Imagine twenty thousand of them breaking into the midst of an European army, confusing the battle plan, overturning carriages, battering the warriors' faces with terrible kicks.

I wish, instead of making proposals about waging war, we could accept a Houyhnhnm proposal to send representatives to help civilize Europe. They could teach us the first principles of honor, justice, truth, self-control, public spirit, hard work, abstinence, friendship, and faithfulness.

Another reason made me hesitate to enlarge his majesty's lands through my discoveries. To tell the truth, I had a few misgivings about how justice is dispensed by princes on such occasions. For instance, imagine a crew of pirates. Driven by a storm, they spy land, go ashore, and rob and plunder. They meet the harmless natives and are treated with kindness. The pirates give the country a new name. They claim it for their king. They murder two or three dozen natives and make off with a couple more, by force. They return home and are pardoned.

So begins a new order, complete with a title and the blessing of God. Ships are sent at the first opportunity. The natives are driven out or destroyed. Their leaders are tortured to reveal the location of their gold. The occupiers have free license to commit acts of inhumanity and lust. The earth reeks with the blood of its inhabitants. And we claim that these butchers are involved in a holy undertaking, to convert and civilize a pagan, cruel people!

This description, I confess, does not apply at all to the British nation. We are an example to the whole world for our wisdom, care, and justice in establishing colonies. We generously support the advancement of religion and learning. We send devout and skilled pastors to spread Christianity. Our representatives are painstaking in distributing justice fairly. Our officials at all levels are well qualified and cannot be corrupted. We send hardworking and upstanding governors who have in mind only the happiness of the people they rule and the honor of the king, their master.

The countries I have described have no desire to be conquered, enslaved, murdered or driven out by colonists. They have no great supplies of gold, silver, sugar, or tobacco. Therefore, I did humbly conclude that the countries I visited were of no interest to us. However, for those who hold another opinion, I am ready to testify, when called, that I was the first European to visit those countries.

As far as taking possession of these lands in my king's name, it never even occurred to me. If it had, considering the various situations I found myself in, it would have made sense to wait for a better opportunity anyway.

Now I have answered the only objection that could ever be raised against me as a travel writer. And so, I here bid farewell to all my courteous readers and return to my little garden. I will keep working to apply the lessons I learned among the Houyhnhnms. I will instruct the yahoos of my own family. I will look at myself in the mirror, as much as possible, until I can tolerate the sight of a human being again. Houyhnhnms are dealt with brutally in my country. I pledge to treat them with respect for the sake of my noble master, his family, his friends, and the whole Houyhnhnm race.

I began last week to permit my wife to sit at dinner with me, at the far end of a long table. I even ask her some questions and tolerate her answers, if they are short. I still consider the smell of a yahoo offensive. I continue to keep my nose stopped-up with strong smelling herbs. Although it is hard for a man to give up old habits, I still hope someday that I will be able to bear the company of a yahoo with no fear of becoming victim to his teeth or his claws.

I could stand yahoos if their only vices were those with which they are born. I am no longer bothered by the sight of a lawyer, a pickpocket, a military man, a fool, a lord, a gambler, a politician, a physician, a witness, a liar, a traitor, or the like. They are part of the natural order. I lose my tolerance, however, when creatures deformed and diseased in body and mind also have an excess of pride. It is pride that drives them to new vices. I will never understand how such an unhealthy animal and so many healthy vices could exist together. The wise and virtuous Houyhnhnms have no word for pride and no terms to describe the evils it inspires. They are not even aware that their own yahoos suffer from pride. But I, with more experience, could plainly observe some simple forms of it among the wild yahoos.

But the Houyhnhnms, who are ruled by reason, are no more proud of their good qualities, than I would be because I am not missing a leg or an arm. I dwell so long on this subject because I want to believe I will yet find an English yahoo whose company I can tolerate. Anyone with the least hint of pride, however, should not bother even entering my sight.

ABOUT THE AUTHOR

A sketch of Jonathan Swift's early life reads like a soap opera. His father, an Englishman living in Ireland, died eight months before Jonathan was born in 1667. When his mother proved financially and emotionally unable to support the family, a rich uncle stepped in to help. Jonathan was turned over to the care of a nurse, who grew so fond of him that she took the baby and ran away with him to England. It was four years before Jonathan returned to Ireland and his uncle's home. Though his kidnapping was only the first of many voyages between England and Ireland, Swift never traveled any further, except in his remarkable imagination.

Jonathan Swift's education and early professional life were filled with disappointment. Although he considered himself an Englishman and very much wanted to attend Oxford

University, he was sent instead at the age of fifteen to Trinity College in Dublin, Ireland. Swift's mischievous nature emerged at Trinity, where he was in frequent trouble over the satires he composed. On one occasion, he had to kneel and apologize to a dean he'd insulted. When he left Trinity, Swift was granted a sub-standard diploma that indicated he had not earned a full college degree.

Despite his failure to apply himself, Swift must have been paying attention in class. The preferred teaching method at Trinity was a kind of debate. Students were given a certain proposition, and then they were supposed to argue its pros and cons. One particular topic was assigned year after year: "Man is a rational animal. No horse is rational. Only rational animals are capable of discipline." Readers of *Gulliver's Travels* and the account of the horses known as Houyhnhnms will discover Swift's views on the question of just who are the rational animals.

Even though he was a mediocre student, Swift was determined to become famous and powerful. Such ambitions were not easily realized in the world of complicated politics in which he lived; in such a difficult time, it was no simple matter to stay on the "right" side. The same year that Swift graduated from college, Great Britain's King James, a Catholic, was forced from his throne. William and Mary, who were Protestants, were crowned in his place. The former king fled to

Ireland, sparking a period of unrest there known as "the Troubles." Unable to continue his studies in Ireland, Swift joined his mother in England. There he began to work as a kind of private secretary for Sir William Temple, a powerful friend of Swift's uncle.

In 1689, Swift experienced his first bout of what we now recognize as Ménière's disease, a disorder of the inner ear that results in intense vertigo, nausea, and headaches. He suffered from the disorder for the rest of his life, with the symptoms worsening as he grew older. When not disabled by his illness, Swift tried several routes to success. He eventually achieved his dream of earning an advanced degree from Oxford, and in 1694, he was ordained as an Anglican priest. He served briefly as a deacon in an isolated Irish town, but he was unhappy in that work, and soon returned to work for William Temple.

When Temple died, he left Swift a hundred pounds and the responsibility for the memoirs he had been writing. Swift published them as Temple had written them, then had to deal with the backlash against some of his employer's unpopular opinions. Swift was criticized for not censoring Temple's autobiography, an idea which angered Swift. It is likely that Swift was remembering this controversy when he later wrote a letter, supposedly by Lemuel Gulliver, complaining bitterly about a censored edition of *Gulliver's Travels*. To soften the satire and avoid offending anyone powerful, Swift's publisher had edited the book's harshest scenes. Swift was furious that his text had been sanitized, and it took ten years before the work was published as he had written it.

In 1700, Swift was named Dean of St. Patrick's Cathedral in Dublin, Ireland, and also received a Doctor of Divinity degree. After that, he was always referred to as Dr. Swift and finally felt that he had achieved some of the prestige he had long desired.

Swift's private life has always been a matter that has puzzled scholars. While working for William Temple, Swift had tutored a child, Esther Johnson, whom he nicknamed Stella. She grew into a beautiful young woman. The exact nature of her relationship with Swift is unknown, but she moved to Dublin in 1701, apparently to be near him. It may be that they were secretly married, but no one knows for sure. Stella died in 1728. When Swift died, a lock of Stella's hair was found among his possessions.

Swift took his position as Dean of St. Patrick's seriously, and eventually got involved in Irish politics. In *Drapier's Letters*, he attacked an English scheme to profit by flooding Ireland with cheap coins. As a result, Swift became an unlikely national Irish hero. He claimed no love for Ireland, declaring, "I am not of this vile country. I am an Englishman." However, he had a "profound hatred of tyranny and oppression." Later, Swift published his most famous satiric essay, "A Modest Proposal" in which the narrator sarcastically suggests solving the problem of poverty in Ireland by selling Irish babies to the rich, to be eaten as delicacies.

As Swift continued to publish, he became well known in literary circles. In 1713, he had formed the "Scriblerus Club" with some of the best-known writers of the day. Their aim was to satirize the work of the thinkers and writers they disliked. The club members decided to ridicule travel books—popular at the time—and it appears Swift was given the job. The work he did became the basis of *Gulliver's Travels*, which was published anonymously in 1726 and became instantly popular. Despite his precautions, Swift's identity as the author of *Gulliver's Travels* was soon widely known.

As Swift aged, his physical problems worsened, and in 1742, he was declared of unsound mind. It has been suggested that Swift's contempt for humanity finally drove him to insanity. It is more likely, however, that Swift's mental decline probably occurred as the result of a catastrophic illness such as a stroke. And there is little evidence in Swift's personal life that he really hated humanity. He liked to say, for instance, that while he disliked the unscrupulous things lawyers did, he liked individual lawyers. Though Swift's physical sufferings could have made him bitter, he remained a compassionate man. Throughout his life, he donated one-third of his income to charity and he spoke out for freedom and against war.

Swift died in 1745, and his self-written epitaph summarizes his life. In death, he wrote, he hoped to find a place "where savage indignation can no longer pierce his heart." Despite his often stinging satire, Swift was always an idealist. His epitaph goes on to challenge those who come after him, saying, "Go traveler, and imitate if you can one who with all his might championed human liberty."

ABOUT THE BOOK

When *Gulliver's Travels* was first published in 1726, Jonathan Swift was living in Ireland. A letter from a friend informed him that his work had created an immediate sensation. The first printing had sold out in less than two weeks. And, in an observation that probably delighted Swift, his friend added how entertaining it was "to hear the different opinions people give of it, though all agree in liking it extremely. . . ." Swift's imaginative masterpiece has been loved ever since, both for its extraordinary story and for its insights into the complexities of human nature.

Gulliver's Travels is, of course, primarily an adventure story. Readers get caught up in such events as Gulliver's assault on the enemy fleet that threatens his Lilliputian friends, his unlikely escape from Brobdingnag, and his narrow escape from the Yahoo savages. Swift also sustains our interest through what we recognize as a common science-fiction technique. He asks a "What if?" question (for example, "What if someone stumbled on a race of giants?") and then inserts enough realistic detail to make the fantastic seem almost possible. Along with adventure, Swift adds a great deal of humor. In addition, *Gulliver's Travels* also has the appeal of an actual travel book, with all the elements of the genuine article: exploits at sea, exotic civilizations, and the danger and excitement of discovery.

Gulliver's Travels pretends to be a straightforward account of Lemuel Gulliver's adventures, but it is actually much more more than that. It is also an intellectual journey. Readers explore the author's ideas about how we live and, by implication, how we *should* live. Swift uses the technique of satire to express those ideas. The satirist criticizes human behavior using humor, but it is a special kind of humor, one based on exaggeration and trickery.

Despite the fact that Swift pretends to be Gulliver, Gulliver and Swift are, in fact, opposites. Jonathan Swift knew things are not always what they seem. He found irony everywhere and had an opinion about almost everything. By contrast, the trusting Gulliver simply sticks to the facts. He describes what he sees, oftentimes in more detail than we would like. But he rarely looks below the surface and hardly ever expresses an opinion. Swift encourages the reader, though, to see many realities that his character Gulliver does not see. For instance, although Gulliver doesn't point it out, we recognize how ridiculous it is for the six-inch-tall emperor of Lilliput to call himself "monarch of all monarchs, taller than the sons of men; whose feet press down to the center of the Earth, and whose head strikes against the sun."

Throughout the book, Swift ridicules humankind's inflated sense of self-importance. But Swift also finds that we possess some redeeming qualities, and he does not condemn us outright. He shows Gulliver acting nobly, especially in Lilliput where his fairness makes the pettiness and cruelty he witnesses seem that much worse. He also shows Gulliver as unfailingly curious, courteous, inventive, and courageous. And Gulliver is not the book's only human being with good qualities. There is also the kindly Captain de Mendez, the first person Gulliver gets to know after returning from Houyhnhnmland. The Captain's generosity and concern for Gulliver show humanity at its best.

In the course of describing Gulliver's travels, Swift finds much about human civilization to condemn and much to admire. He recognizes there are few absolute truths and many exceptions to every general rule. In Lilliput, the first country that Gulliver visits, we see the human race in miniature. The Lilliputians are brave, charming, clever, and unfailingly polite, but they also reveal pettiness, backbiting, cruelty, and excessive pride.

In the second country visited, Brobdingnag, we examine humans at close range and again find a mix of good and bad. The Brobdingnagians are at once gross and unfeeling and noble. The table manners of the giants, though no different than ours, disgust Gulliver and readers who see through his eyes. Gulliver witnesses a terrible public execution, stays to the bitter end, and describes every detail down to the height of the spurting blood.

He is repulsed and fascinated; so is the reader. Some of the giants are cold-hearted, such as Gulliver's first owner, whose efforts to profit from putting Gulliver on display nearly kill him. On the other hand, the Queen displays goodwill toward Gulliver. Glumdalclitch, Gulliver's tender nurse, is a warm-hearted girl. And the King's understanding of politics is both profound and moral.

In the third country visited, Houyhnhnmland—its name is supposed to sound like the whinnying of a horse—we examine the human race from the viewpoint of superior reason. In the view of Gulliver's master there—a horse—humans are exactly like the deplorable Yahoos, with one difference: their refusal to *use* their ability to reason makes them worse than Yahoos. Analyzing human civilization, Gulliver's master describes its many weaknesses. As a result, Gulliver sees humanity through Houyhnhnm eyes and turns against the human race. When Gulliver returns to England, he aspires to be a Houyhnhnm, and he is barely able to be in the same room with his wife and children, preferring the company of his own horses. As the story comes to a close, Gulliver is slowly becoming more human again, though he still has great contempt for his own species.

Gulliver's darkened view of humankind could certainly be a natural response to having spent time with the honorable Houyhnhnms. It would be easy to despise any society that did not meet their high standards. However, while the Houyhnhnms have many admirable traits, they are far from perfect. Though they live in harmony, their lives are rather boring. They have no names, no individual identities. Reason helps the Houyhnhnms avoid many of the pitfalls of humans, but they also lack our passion and our compassion. They are as cold-hearted about the proposal to exterminate the Yahoos as the Lilliputians were about blinding and starving Gulliver.

Swift provides no final view of human nature. But it might safely be said that *Gulliver's Travels* leaves us with the sense that we cannot depend completely on any one particular philosophy or government. Perhaps we need, instead, to rely more on the very thing the Houyhnhnms lack: our ability to feel joy, love, and compassion for others.